CEDRIC'S TRUTH
The Kids On Sturtevant Street

(A Novel by a Musician)

BILL BANFIELD

Copyright © 2018 Bill Banfield
All rights reserved
First Edition

PAGE PUBLISHING, INC.
New York, NY

First originally published by Page Publishing, Inc. 2018

ISBN 978-1-64138-547-3 (Paperback)
ISBN 978-1-64138-548-0 (Digital)

Printed in the United States of America

"…Russell Woods was the center of a solid community that nurtured its children's desire to explore the world.

Cedric's Truth is a composite of Bill Banfield's formative years on Sturtevant, a street that we shared as neighbors. The many sounds of Detroit ring clear in his rendition of a young musician, persistent in the search for his voice, his truth…"

Hilda Vest, former Editor, Broadside Press, Detroit, Mich.

"…What if music was life itself, a life in search of truth every minute and every measure of each day? And what happens when that quest takes place in a world that's hard of hearing? Meet Cedric Sullivan, a beautiful, complicated, enigmatic character who tries to negotiate this world carrying the wisdom of his ancestors, the knowledge of the streets, and the inner turmoil of the artist. Evocative of Ralph Ellison, Hermann Hesse, and Henry Dumas, Bill Banfield's debut novel takes us on a journey rich with tragi-comic twists and turns, flights of passion and philosophical meditations, and a remarkable cultural history of late 20th century America. This book will open your eyes and your ears. Dig it…"

Robin D. G. Kelley, author of Thelonious Monk: The Life and Times of an American Original

Henry Louis Gates has written of his workings …

"…Composer and musicologist Bill Banfield is one of the most original voices on the scene today…he tunes readers in to the conversations happening worldwide between the notes of contemporary musical culture. Not only do his musings help us make sense of the places and periods of change across generations, from jazz to hip-hop, the Harlem Renaissance to Cuba; they remind us that we each play a part, as makers, producers, listeners, or consumers, in the symphony of expression marking the beats of our journey here on earth."

Henry Louis Gates, Jr.
Alphonse Fletcher University Professor, Harvard University

Cedric's Truth is a story about music, blackness, history, politics, and an artist's devotion to his craft. It is a novel about the tortured road of a musician teetering between genius and madness, and it is a meditation on the difficulty of making sense of and peace with the past. Told in a series of lively vignettes, this is a romantic portrait of a place and a people, a gripping record of a life lived tragically, outrageously, and brilliantly, and a score that accompanies the journey of a musician "following the melody of his soul."

Emily Bernard, author, editor, Remember Me To Harlem;
The Letters of Langston Hughes and Carl Van Vechten

Inspirational Thanks

To all my mentors, living or otherwise, and to those whose stories I've borrowed.

To Anne and Bill Banfield, my parents, who always talked to me and guided me, who gracefully embraced life and beyond, and whose marriage of over sixty-three years inspires us all.

To Harold Cruse.

To the Reverend Charles G. Adams.

To the Reverend Drs. Ray and Gloria Hammond, Lori, Marty, Lynn, and Devonne.

Thanks to my punctilious friend and editor, Vicky Rodriguez. Without you, this novel would not stand.

Thanks to John and Serena Wright for regarding me with "deep love, but limited tolerance." I'm proceeding with caution.

Finally, thanks to countless inspiring and warring characters who have challenged me to think and act creatively and constructively.

Many, many thanks.

".... I think that the majority of musicians are interested in truth. If you play a musical statement and if it's a valid statement, that's a truth right there in itself. All musicians are striving for as near to a certain perfection as they can get, that's a truth right there... so in order to play those kinds of things, to play truths, you got to live as much truth as you can."

John Coltrane

Cover Painting by James Zeke Tucker

This novel is dedicated to the woman
who gave me the name Cedric.
For my mother, and Dad too, who gave me
direction, love, and the ice cream story.

"... In a government culture takeover where evil intentions attempt to deceive, mute and distort truth, and blatantly attack arts, people and progress, it becomes incumbent on every thinking artist to resist evil regimes and bring to such suffocated times a spirit of love, truth(s) and unrestricted voice so people can be lifted and illuminated. To "be an artist" as cliche as it is made to sound sometimes, is an act of freeing truth. In that is rebellion, courage, care and a profound sound of universality of expression that makes living matter respond. If that is simply released the results are incalculable. "Expression" frees souls, lifts...That becomes the mantra..."

Cedric

New York, Summer 2012: Dinner With a Friend

I have to wonder about myself sometimes, whether I'm crazy or I'm just operating as body, mind frozen, and passing through on exhaustion or on auto drive.

I look at you across the table and you seem to be handling your life just fine. I mean, you've seen me here before, but no, this time I'm done, end of the road. I just haven't figured out yet if there are other forks in it, but the bumps and bruises I have have been my best company on this roll. When I leave here today? I don't know where I'm landing, somewhere in America. I know you say you live "on an island off the coast of the US called New York, and America, you don't go in there." But, come on, the Midwest isn't all that bad! It has space and I need space to feel and breathe my ideas. You know I love to travel. I love moving, different landscapes. Can't stay in one place, though, that's why I can't find real love. When love comes knocking, it finds an empty room because the renter moved to another location before the coffee even got brewing.

Lately I've been running from that embarrassing and sad stunt at the college, that attempt to reconcile myself to faded dreams. But you know what else? It's been a beautiful roll.

Tonight, I'm having dinner with my dear friend, enjoying a glass of wine, sitting here with you, and I'm going to tell you who I have been trying hard to become.

I love life. I love my dreams and the cultivation, the pursuit of ideas. I love who I have wanted to become. I love people, and I love young people. I was born a teacher. I was born to be a musician, I was born to be an explorer. I am primarily a creative dreamer, always on active duty, on call 25/8.

"So why do you keep running, who are you trying to find?" you ask.

I'm looking for me! I'm like the visible invisible man. I think people hear me, but they don't see my insides sometimes. Oh, there's some sun in there, it's just the Blues and the funk out here that mucks everything up! I myself am the keeper of the vineyards of my own mind.

Really, friend, look: I've tried all my life to stay positive, focused, energized, and I have had all the right reasons but… well, I'm staying positive for you right now. What are you ordering? Everything you do makes sense on any plate. Me? God! I'm an ordered mess. I like my tastes all mixed up. If the special is Bluefish and asparagus with mustard on the side, I order the asparagus taken off, a side of carrots, sautéed onions, and garlic mashed potatoes, rice with a side of soy sauce. My coffee drink? Caramel hazelnut latte, baby!

And look at you. That dress is gorgeous! Everything on your body is always order-right. *My* fashion codes are messed up: ironed dress shirt, jeans, crumpled sports jacket, mismatched socks, and my polished leather loafers. And I don't care if the music is Miles, then country, then Bach, I just like the sounds to keep coming, allowing different turns at every tune. Yep, I've gotten complex on you, but I'm not complicated or conflicted yet.

Of course you can read me, but you have to sit with me for a while. I'm a good read, a real story, friend!

Why am I tripping? There are a few things that really get you in trouble in life: when you willingly hurt someone, rub up against power the wrong way, or when you move toward truth. You know what really got me thinking the other day? What would happen if we all stopped once in a while and let another team drive the wagon for a few? Then we get to begin again at another point on a different road. On your job, it would be just a shift of teams. All your problems would be resolved by the other guy, who saw the end of your road as the springboard for their journey. This way you'd never reach a dead end, somebody else would just take over. Now that's a life with some possibilities, some decent friggin' chances!

You want to know something else I've thought about recently? What if God were watching us, holding a note in his or her hand? What if your note was a compilation of right moves, and she'd hand it to you as a map for the rest of your life? What if that map was part of a plan to guide you, what if this map only took the good you've done into account, and what if for every misstep you got three fruitful options because you already paid the price for your mistake? Think about it… you get three more for every failed or attempted step. You'd be an active agent for your moves, but God gets to decide the endings. Now that's a good religion!

I'm a religious person when the religion works out for me. I know that's funny, but I'm not the only one who hopes like that. Were you all religious in your family? I'm the the only one left. That's me, myself, and I: Cedric, the one who keeps on searching. I'm tired, friend. I need a pillow to catch my head. I really appreciate you for just being here to hear.

Prelude: On Mom and Coffee

There were many mornings in those old days I would slip down real early to see Mom.

You could smell the warm coffee that had already been brewing and you could hear the smooth pour of the half and half cream she used, but no sugar. The back stairs that led up from the kitchen snaked up two flights and around walls, channeling the aroma that crept under bedroom doors and summoned me. I awakened regularly and crawled away and out of my dreams in a mummy-like stagger, creeping slowly, stumbling down the stairs to see Mom and have a talk. Just me and she. As I reached the kitchen, she had already been there, I would bet, by five in the morning. I would find her in the dining room, lights off, quietly sitting in her favorite chair. She would be there, just sipping her coffee. I would always ask her the same childishly inquisitive and rhetorical question, "Mom, what are you doing?" The answer was consistent: "I'm having my coffee, baby." That early-morning cup of coffee and the silence of the room where she sat, queenly, came to mean for me reflection and clarity.

I am sure of it now, my mother's morning coffee was her clarity concoction, and the moments of order that she squeezed away to herself, sitting early way before the day's business began, was how she claimed clarity. In those days, Mom would have had it all worked out long before my small ashy feet hit the kitchen floor, or Dad shaved.

I am coming to think that clarity is getting through the world around you, and you inside of yourself working in that world; clarity means you are allowed to see clearly through and under the doors, widows, that allow you to reach the seats assembled there, on the other side, for you to rest. Understanding yourself, following your faith, your goals; taking time to be caring and reflective, being set in your soul about your identity and whom and what you love in this life: that is clarity.

I'm pretty sure now that the word and the tones left to reflect what we see and know are as valuable as a anything we leave here standing to represent us and the story of life as we live.

Some are called to be square in the middle of that creative sharing thing called music, art. Those spend their lives with this, and all along the way lots of sounds and joy are made and people are moved. That movement of the soul, that joy, can be life-sustaining and life-changing. It's still changing mine. People are greatly moved by music, really moved, so I figured I'd try to have my life shaped by that moving in our world. That's all I was trying to do. That's all I ever wanted to do. That was finding my truth, sitting and having my coffee. Why, then, would they try to stop this? That's what always gets me in the end.

Russell Woods

"Tell us why you think our generation looks at things so differently. Mrs. Anderson, what happened that night?"

A group of students from the local Moses O'Neal College circle Mrs. Anderson on her front porch with recorders, film going, and busily ask her questions. They have been assigned this project following the college disturbance, which took place nearly 2 years ago, where Cedric, her former student, was arrested following that community lecture and debate. The students, some of who were there, will return several times and Mrs. Anderson will tell the story, retelling what happened that night and sharing her wisdom.

"Now, Russell Woods in Detroit was a Black neighborhood that was lined with beautiful homes, well-cut grass and trees, kids playing in the streets. There was a park with swings, art and music festivals, and ice cream trucks that lined the streets, waiting for the kids to come running out after school. Doug, Peter, Kristy, Michael, Roy, Gregg, Wendy, Thomas, Maria, Linda, Ricky, Keith, Shanita, Carl, Bobby, Angie, Stephen, Stephanie, Mary, Darlene, Michael, Alison, Annie, Kathy, Jimmy, Brock, and of course, Cedric. These were all the kids on Sturtevant Street. Isn't that funny? No Shanekwas, Mileks, Ka-vasees, or Kwames. Winterhalter School and Birney Elementary were the public grade schools that graduated these urban youth to middle and high schools that shaped those kids into well-rounded adults. Again, I say this proudly, Detroit was a great place where Black people looked beautiful.

CEDRIC'S TRUTH: THE KIDS ON STURTEVANT STREET

"Black people were hard, too. Your uncle on the East side wasn't from your side of town, but he was in your family and those East side first cousins could have ended up being "bad," in jail, or dead. But all this was a part of everybody's reality and the wonderful complexity of Black folks' lives. There seemed to be options, various viewpoints, and many mirrors to look in and dream through."

Most of the students who are assembled on Mrs. Anderson's porch are now enthralled with the old woman, but perhaps they are just patient enough to tolerate her, for the assignment. Mrs. Anderson's meandering tale goes on.

"The parents tried to keep up the idea that the kids on Sturtevant Street in Russell Woods were going to be "somebodies." They would have been oh, four, five years old when Malcolm X got shot in '65 and probably heard nothing of it. And I guess they were all about seven or eight in 1968 when Martin Luther King was assassinated. I certainly remember the mood of the country then, but Russell Woods was a bubble that the kids on Sturtevant Street thought was a mirror of the whole Black world. It wasn't. They should have known better. Our neighborhood was not far from the boundaries of struggle that most know as the reality of, what do you all call it, the hood. But all the "hood kids" and all the Russell Woods kids went to the same schools, so the reality was that most of them knew all the sides to the modern Black urban tale, but they had choices and privileges. I'm sure many young people got their butts whooped after school by those tough kids, but somehow I don't remember that as being anything but the reality of the world, diverse in its balances, fair in its allowing you to make a decision and yet still full of promise if you worked hard."

Mrs. Anderson continues her sharing, always insisting on how good life was back then on Sturtevant Street. "That's what we taught young people. In school there were no guns, just fists and bad kids who lived on the other side of the nicely kept lawns. All these kids bought candy from the same candy, pop, potato chips, and Honey Bun stores, owned by some Greek or Caldean family. Now and Laters, Mary Janes, Twisters, Pork Rinds, Hawaiian Punch, Superior Potato Chips, Vernors and Faygo Punch Pop, those were all the staple junk foods of the day for the kids on Sturtevant Street.

Zachekius Washington is a sophomore, dressed in a hooded Old Navy sweat shirt, white, clean Phat Farm Classic gymies. He is bright with ambition yet dedicated to the causes, the languages, and the zeal of his generation. He runs a website, *Call It Out Now*, where he hosts an online news show, poetry reads, and announces his "soul food messages jams." He is a born entrepreneur, majoring in political science. He hangs a Tupac poster over the bed in his dorm room and reads Malcolm's *Speeches to Young People, The Ballot or the Bullet*, and yes, watches *The Bill Murray Show*. He interrupts Mrs. Anderson's narration.

"Hi, Mrs. Anderson, pleasure is mine. My name is ZW. You know, I'm trying to be 'bout and 'bout it." Zachekius unapologetically comments, "Mrs. Anderson, just being real, it's difficult for me to connect to these people. They don't sound like anyone I know, maybe my mom's and them, way back in the day. Black people back then just don't seem normal to me, made up on TV or something."

Mrs. Anderson turns directly to ZW, glaring indignantly. "What do you mean? The kids on Sturtevant Street were very normal kids. I think it was integration that robbed people of a whole lot of self-sustaining stuff, where people looked out and took care of one another. I assure you, young man, none of these folks and their lives were made up on TV. That new Cosby-ism, the post-civil rights prizes, had so many folks racing into Made-it Land, erased family memory or something, but that has also left lots of folks, even around here, still in the economic gutter. We can't blame your generation for running after all the goodies and forgetting about those good-ol'-days values, 'cause you are mainly now just living on the goodies that those times passed into in your laps, and therein lies the problem."

Another student, Patricia Paris, pushes. "How did Cedric fit into all this?"

Mrs. Anderson sighs, takes the rubber band out of her hair, letting it hang down as if to suggest that this one will need some explaining.

"Well, let's see, Cedric Sullivan was one of the kids on Sturtevant Street. I remember a story his father once told me. When Mr. Sullivan was a little boy, his mother gave him money to go to the drugstore on the corner, and he wanted to have some vanilla ice cream. That was it! But the ol' white drugstore man wouldn't let him buy the ice cream he wanted. "Little chocolate boy," he told Mr. Sullivan, "you don't want vanilla ice cream; you want chocolate ice cream." "No, sir, I want vanilla ice cream," Mr. Sullivan said to him. That ol' white man said to him again, "Little chocolate boys only eat chocolate ice cream," and wouldn't let him buy the ice cream he wanted! Cedric's father never ate chocolate ice cream again because he wasn't gonna let that old white man keep him from getting what he wanted." Mrs. Anderson giggles and slaps her knee, then sighs and seems to sober up. "Cedric's father is gone now, but he and Cedric's mother, who claimed they were "children of the Depression," lived full lives. That's the kind of people Cedric came from. I close my eyes, hard-pressed to remember, pulling from these images, words, scenes, experiences that unlock these stories for you all. But I'll tell you, these days, nobody cares about the normal stuff anymore, like lessons and them ol'-time values."

Zach, now fired up, speaks in his impatient air, as if the world won't stop, begin, or keep going fast enough without him being in it. He clearly wants no more of the old woman's anecdotes. "Mrs. Anderson, we came here to get a real sense of where we should go. You have to *feel* us on this tip. Our generation knows the game and we don't like the players either. It's time for us to flip the script on 'em! Brothers and sisters today are coming together around the issues and using the system to figure it out on our time. Seems like those Black players who say they are in play, hey, like my mom's and them, should be moving on down the line, let us step in. But you know, they aren't having it, because they still want to make it all good for them. So they send us off to college to learn stuff that was useful for them back in the day, but I'm looking to cash in on 'em— "It's all 'bout them Benjamins, baby." And if you take a real deep peep at all the high rollers, that's their roll, and hey, it's all their take. So I'm seeing "values" as the lessons we see "in the real", and adapting to the environment. That's values, that's got value!! I mean, that's the real roll, right? That's what Cedric was probably getting to."

His haughtiness takes her breath away. He's only been here born and living for three minutes and hasn't spit on the ground two and a half times yet. What did he know? She'd say, "that's how these young people think, that it's all about them and their "roll on" today."

Mrs. Anderson is visibly irritated, irked by his arrogance yet feeling his passion. She's beginning to swelter in the 90-degree summer heat, and she swats away a mosquito, as aggravated with the weather as she is with this young whippersnapper.

"Young man, you sound angry! Naw, naw, naw now! You can't get to truth by being angry. Being angry is just a condition. If you live your life just expecting negative results, you will find yourself swimming in a pool of negativity. Believe in your capacity to create a good space over the evil and take hold of all the good life has in store for you.

"You see, Cedric was someone who believed in the beauty of the human soul, but he lost his faith trying to find his truth."

She pauses, then continues, looking past him as if she hasn't heard him.

"I am giving up my daytime TV stories to be with you all today, because *All My Children in The Storms* is where I have been living for the last thirty years." She giggles to herself. "I really do appreciate you all choosing to take the time to do this, come over and talk with me. I am not on the Internet! You can't Google me, this is real. I am the original *keeping it real*." She laughs and slaps her leg. "You all have to be aimed and have your game plan to make good on this world. You have so many tools but you are lacking the ideas about what you are supposed to be doing. Nowadays everything is a program that somebody else set, and I know you all aren't liking who set the programs up, nor the reasons either. Everything is all too quick, too "push button and pass the Benjamin," as you say Zach. I may be an old woman now, but what I knew then and what I hope for now shouldn't be that far from y'all.

"You see, young people, we never had a Black college near us up North like the Moses O'Neal College. To think, somebody founded a college to train Black Southern migrants in business or the humanities, my Lord, my God. I mean, the students there that evening that you all are asking about heard some new things as far as I could tell. And my goodness Lord, young people turned out that evening like a flood of witnesses! I saw you all raised up, standing on your feet cheering. That's what Cedric was missing of late, that's why he came there that night. I'll tell you how I saw it."

Mrs. Anderson's Story: The Last Lecture

"It happened on a Thursday evening, a few days before the end of the semester when we were all hoping for a start of a good late Spring and summer. Some of you kids were there. The college president, in his fashion, welcomed all of the guests gathered there in Beck Hall.

"Good evening everybody. We at Moses O'Neal College appreciate all the support and excitement for this evening's event and our esteemed guests. Popular culture debate is important work for us here. It connects as part of the tissue, the meaning of what and who is impactful to our students' lives. We don't have any doubt nor do we try to excuse it away, popular culture, its presence is major. It's essential to the discussion of what is the buzz, the identity, the character and the future of the society we live in."

President Summers, dressed a bit sloppily as usual, was out of pitch with the elegance and dress of the hall he stood in. For some reason, this hall with its theater-in-the-round seating, red velour drapes, and state-of-the-art lighting, was set more for drama than lecture that night. He continued his introduction.

"Popular culture is problematic, exciting, complicated, important and fun. In education, how we decide to dissect the questions, issues, calls for a broad minded group, a sensitive group and an informed group with insights. Presumably, all of our guests love music, watch TV, and use the Internet. They're plugged in, wired, fired up, and ready to go!" He laughs louder than the audience does. "This evening we have our own professor Miles Brown, and joining him, esteemed writers, teachers, leaders from the community who will share their ideas with each other and with us tonight. Please, may I introduce our moderator, community activist, and, as she stressed I mention, "mother and mentor" Dr. Sharon Strong, who will introduce our four panelists."

You could feel the excitement in the hall resonating in red. We anticipated something rich and community-connected from the college. Cedric did too, I guess.

There were nearly a hundred people there, and we applauded. Sharon Strong walked onto the stage: she was middle-aged, nicely grayed, very full-figured, and attractive; she was dressed in a blue business suit, top wrapped in a blue-and-yellow scarf. She spoke in a stately, attractively low, slow, steady voice. She put her glasses on, drank from a cup placed beneath the podium, and addressed the guests.

"Good evening. I am so grateful to President Summers and the Moses O'Neal College community. Too often the colleges and universities do their thing, which is, well, a very great thing, but they do it in isolation, cut off from the community. But not this institution! You stay cemented and connected to the peoples' lives, which spring from the streets of this city, this neighborhood, this state.

"We are a better community because of your presence and your contributions. This evening, we have, in addition to your own professor Miles Brown, recognized arts-activist, TV news anchor, our very own, Kristy Kilson; the righteous Doctor Reverend Justin Simpson from Zion United Methodist; and Dr. Larry Johnson, professor of sociology from our neighboring Grant College. Now, we have plenty of people running around appearing on TV, talking and quaking about pop music, and making the Band and all this noise about this and that." The audience laughed. "But we also have knowledgeable, passionate, and informed people who care about these things."

She read the title of the evening's debate."Tonight's topic of discussion is Popular Culture and Its Relation to Our Contemporary

Grounding and Shaping: What are the Questions We Should Be Asking?

"I want to begin by asking our panel this evening about the recent show phenomenon, *American Idol*. How should we read this highly popular music TV show? Some have suggested that it represents a new wave of more common-culture variety show-entertainment, which has, for many observers, been a very positive national phenomenon. What is your response to this positive take on the show?"

You could see the sea of faces wondering who would be the first to "take us to the water to drink." The silence, after some thought, was reluctantly broken. Rev. Justin Simpson, typical local preacher-type, relatively quick to respond, grabbed the table mic, cleared his throat and fell right in.

"Well, a recent *US Today* op piece drew attention to the pluses of American Idol. At the center of this debate is the question of an outmoded critique, that we have lost a certain "musical values set" in the popular culture market place. The criteria for what constitutes worthy commercial artistry has fallen to an all time low, I believe. I see *American Idol* as a "commercial boxed lunch." I don't find it helpful to cultivating a new generation of would-be commercial artists. Our real challenge today is the fight against the pervasiveness of market-forced culture which runs counter, it seems, to individuality, deeper expression, or originality. Secondly, *American Idol* breeds commercial emptiness. My response is not so positive and I blame Hollywood for this kind of overall decline."

There was muttering, some *umm*'s, some head shakes in the crowd. Something was brewing already.

Dr. Larry Johnson, professor type, in his mid-fifties, with a more-than-polished highbrow tone, reached for the microphone and pulled it towards himself to counter.

"I find such a position untenable. This kind of attack is just another expression of fogeyism. I *am* older than the reverend here, but that position has been heard as long as there has been popular culture. Throughout history, there have similar complaints about the emergence of the new music, from minstrelsy to ragtime to blues, to jazz to R&B, Elvis and rock'n'roll, and all these have risen from the same sounds, movements, popular market idols in popular culture. These are simply American cultural upsurges; we've seen them all before and I don't see any need for concerns. There is no difference, besides the young people know all the rules."

Kristy Kilson was actually a kid from Sturtevant Street. You didn't know that, huh? She always dressed very corporate, hair pulled back and in a bun. She was always tight, prissy, and about herself. She didn't grab the mic, no sir, she motioned for the gentleman to place it before her.

"I read that piece as well, Professor, and I have to say, it does makes a convincing argument for the pluses of *American Idol*. I mean, it reaches 32 million homes, which compares to *The Ed Sullivan Show* of the 1950's, and, like *The Sullivan Show*, it launches careers. This show cuts across the American gender, social, racial, and generational divides. Consider the democratic nature of the participation, which is healthy, and falls right in with the Americanist themes which we are hearing a lot about in wartime. Initially, as I understand it, anyone can try out, and the winners are ultimately chosen by the viewing audience. This brings the nation around a single bonding focus, and it encapsulates the American dream of instant celebrity."

Moderator Dr. Strong joined in forcibly, clearly not a fan. I'm sure all this tension stirred within us an unease which was the stage for what was coming.

"OK, sounds really fantastic. My question is: all this at what cost, and for what? In terms of costs, the show and the winners are making bundles of money; it *is* the entertainment business, this is nothing new or shocking. But what are we looking to, to be an "Idol"? Is this artistry at all innovative or original?"

Rev. Simpson jumped back in, defending his initial displeasure with the show.

"The quality of the talent is amateur in most cases. At best, this is a hi-tech, big budget talent contest. It creates and feeds into a "push button, pick the flavor of the month" mentality. And anyway, half the kids sing out of tune. They should come and join one of our choirs here at the church; our rehearsals are every Wednesday night!"

He laughed along with the audience.

Kristy Kilson motioned for the mic again, one swift glance being enough to spur her all-too-quick-to-accommodate panel of gentlemen into action.

"Well, the show *is* attempting to represent a full cultural make up, but I think the show of ethnic artistry on the program is boxed and narrow, so I am suspicious."

Dr. Johnson joined in again. "I think at the center of the American popular mythology lies the narrative of race intrigue. Our social and class prescription; the values of the world of the powerful and the common person, and how this gets represented. Many times the designated carriers symbolic of these ideas are our idols. But here, we have this TV-projected and constructed "heroes of the common folk": Miss America, Superman, Shaft, doesn't matter, we don't get it here in America served up in any other way except what gets baked up there in Hollywood! So there is a lot at stake here with playing the game of *American Idol*. Again, it loses on several grounds for me."

Professor Miles Brown motioned for the mic and gestured as if to remind students they should be saying something. "OK, I've been quiet. But I think after considering the relevance of these critiques, we need to continue to be open, patient, even though we may all be growing older and less hip these days. So, I say, let's keep waiting for that surge of new and promising talent the network executives promise is worth being our American Idol."

Moderator Dr. Strong asked, "What do you all think, *really* think about all the fuss around the images and language of hip hop culture? It certainly adds fire to the questions you all have been addressing about the effect of popular culture. Professor Brown?"

"The social, cultural impact, the pervasiveness of hip hop culture is impossible to miss. We would all agree. It could be said to be the most influential music culture style today. Its economic-entrepreneurial effects, while at the end of the day controlled by white business interests, are really, in immediate entrepreneurial and creative navigation, in the hands of young Black people."

The audience clapped wildly for their favorite teacher and local campus hero. Now, during all this exchange with these folks talking, everybody had been perking up , their buttons were being pressed. The interest went up another notch with this new topic, and I noticed Professor Brown had knocked over his glass of water to get back to the mic.

"Yeah, yeah. They have generated more capital from and within the arts entertainment industry than any other generation of artists. I wonder, though, is this necessarily a good thing? Lord knows, these young artists' messages are, well, Lord only knows." The audience laughed.

Kristy Kilson joined in. She let her hair down and got real with the audience for a moment, dropping her tidy news anchor persona. "In our neighborhood, you were expected to grow up and be all you could be. But me, I wasn't caught up in that at all. So I was always on the outside; in church, in school, at home. I was no sweet little Susie in my classes!" She chuckled and soft laughter rippled through the audience. "So, hip hop for me, and yeah it's kind of *ghetto*, as they call it, but that's me too. When I listen to this music, I can smell flexing muscles, I can feel the energy bursting from legs waiting to move with the beat. There's a welling up of a kind of, I don't know, some ancient African dance we all want to be about. These messages are well beyond the words; I can smell, feel, taste a righteous rebelliousness that, if the music was anymore palatable for older folks, or for, excuse me, the plain pedestrian white adults, I wouldn't want it. It's that side of us, and these younger folks, too, that senses in this music a real rise that if all else is defined by others, then this music must be my definition of the real me. That's what the beat does for you. It grounds you. That beat is really elemental, essential, it's— ubiquitous. I mean, I can even excuse the boyish stupidity present in the music that is mad at all girls, when artists call us the "b" word. That doesn't bother me much. Men have always been stupid and lacked the brains and the good sense to be respectful to women, truly. And I expect that today, any strong young lady would easily flip a disrespectful word right back at 'em. I certainly did, and they didn't teach me that on our block neither. But these artists' music is powerful in this way. Hip hop is arresting, psychologically, like nothing else we've heard before. Through reaching into hip hop culture we can go a long way toward understanding our youth, the times, technologies of expression. I believe we can be better in the face-off and fend off the attack and hopelessness in contemporary culture as Black people."

The audience resonated with her words, and they broke out into wild cheers and copious applause. Dr. Strong then broke in to engage the audience.

"Alright, let me pose a few targeted questions to this audience. I have a general suspicion, knowing many members in this audience, that you all are not yet moved to engage us, because we haven't hit it quite yet? So…"

The students began to come to the microphones at the front of the auditorium. Something began to happen as the discussion passed into the hands of the audience. It changed the dynamic in the room.

ZW, you were there. You were the first one to step up. "Hi, I'm ZW, Zach Washington. You all—oh, but not you, Miss Kilson. I mean, you're on it. I got all love for you, I mean, well, you know. But like I was saying, the rest of you just take for granted the cultural critique put out there every day by artists who feel the heat and who respond with spits and rhymes that do the proper analysis by replicating an important cultural dynamic that addresses what the real issues are! Even in this racist society, white people still don't get it. Most of what gets done is all for them, they don't mean *me* when they talk about their ideas for a great society.

"It's great everywhere I look, except where there are some of me there! *American Idol*, iPods, I mean, who cares? It's just another trick and posturing of White America, and mostly behind a bunch of smiling faces and trick bags."

Another audience member, a white male student, stepped up to the mic to speak. "Hi, I'm Jeremy Ruban. It's always "race" this and "the white man" that. There's more to what's going on than just the racial issues. It always goes there and there's more to this talk than just that. We live in an American America, man! There are millions of white, red, *green* people even, I don't know, but all I hear in these talks is race, race, race. *That* to me is being racist. Racist is when you force the issue and make it all about your race. I don't see it as any trick. I mean, yeah, there are a lot of dudes, man, who foul up the whole thing with their greed and all. But it isn't just a white man's thing. It's a *man's* thing."

Now, Ms. Patricia Paris here, you came up to the mic with a quiet, forceful fire. "It's a *man's* thing?! Neither of you, nor any of the gentlemen on the panel, addressed within this discussion the idea of a missed moment to achieve equality, representation, from a *woman's* point of view. The TV ads are completely saturated with female imagery, nothing but things to lure us into buying some more shit, excuse me, but really!" Patricia stopped to catch her breath and continued her diatribe. "I am so sick of TV's codes for what beauty is. Not only are *American Idol* or Hollywood's shows a travesty in commercialism, it really *is* a white woman's beauty show, a show where *I* wasn't invited to participate or judge. The Black woman's face has gone from Aunt Jemima to a minute of victory only as an option by giving Black men a little play, an Oprah moment every now and then. But we've gone to total invisibility, especially now with so much interracial dating and marriage, and get this: Black men and women of other races now form the favored picture. Black women have been left to the left of the frame!"

All the ladies in the audience immediately gave her a standing ovation. "Go ahead, sista!" But then, a man approached the mic slowly. His voice broke into the familiar sounds of the banter and intellectualism we'd slowly grown friendly with for the previous hour.

"May I say a few words? The only people who have touched on anything relevant or real are the young audience members, who seem to really be on it. However, I need to say something, from very deep within."

Lord, Lord goodness, goodness that voice, that voice… Oh, that "deep within." He slowly, deliberately, and very dramatically brought the mic towards himself. I couldn't see his face at that point, but *that voice*, and, although I hadn't seen him in over twenty five years, since he was a kid, I knew then it was Cedric.

As he approached the front and the light shone on him, I could see he was holding a gun, pointing it at his own head. Somebody screamed. One could only guess that the security guards were on a round far on the other side of the college in order to have missed the shriek. Cedric was dressed in a ratty, ruffled suit, a dirty white shirt, and loosened necktie; he carried a clipboard under his other arm, on which he had probably been taking notes. A classic tattered high school history teacher uniform. I think he had heard of the success of Professor Miles' union of the community, the various colleges linking with the O'Neal Cultural Center, and the discussion with all these young people. I think the word got out and that is what drew him there that night. In many ways I soon learned he admired professor Miles, saw him as an extension of what he could only dream of setting in motion. All the panelists, trying to stay calm for the sake of their students' safety, were dazed. Cedric cleared his throat in the mic, which was calming despite the situation, then spoke.

"There's only one thing I need from you all tonight. And Mr. President, please, just tell everyone to sit tight for a moment, and I'll be very quick with this. I just have a few things I want to share."

President Summers asked everyone in his practiced authoritative voice, "Please, everybody, let's just be calm for a moment and do as he says for now." Nobody moved, strangely enough. Surreal that we were in a college auditorium and the reality of the outer world, which stopped, had suddenly grabbed us by the throat.

Cedric continued.

"I am not here to take any possession, nor to hurt anybody. I only ask you indulge me a few moments in this short time of reflection. I came here to be connected to this community of thinking, caring people, because, well, out there nobody cares and nobody is thinking about anything except for their own needs, it seems. It drives me nutty.

"My name is Cedric Sullivan and I belong here tonight."

Kristy Kilson called out, "Cedric, is that you?"

"Yes, it's me, Kristy." He continued. "You know what's so interesting to me about tonight, rattles my soul? Is that each one of you, you gate-keepers, all represent a piece of what I have come to question and to dislike deeply, and what I hate to love but what I love to hate. So I'm suspicious of you, except for what I hope for and see in these young bright minds. Ironically, so many of my dreams have been shaken by what you do and represent. Sound confused, maybe?

I'm still working it out, just my trip though. Thanks for the journey. You professor, tell me, what must we do to be saved? Preacher man, Reverend, sermon us.

"Where do I tune in, whose community is mine? Ms. Community, mentor, mother, Dr. Strong?" He laughed in admiration, it seemed. "Dr. Johnson? It's disingenuous, I think, to claim on the one hand you believe in young people and on the other hand you set no real mechanisms or parameters for them to survive in a world where you create all the rules. And Kristy, my dear sister, how are you? It's been so and too long. Our blessed street has proven its rich soil to have flowered such a prize. You are so beautiful, just the way I remembered you. It's been so long."

Kristy Kilson simply hung there, speechless, sporting the most frightened expression, as if she had been waiting for this moment, this time to reconnect or something, but not in this way. What did this mean?

Cedric spoke as if it were his last chance to make someone see.

"All my life, I worked to be recognized by your establishment, thinking my work would contribute in all sorts of ways. My parents, community, church, school all provided me with everything everybody said we should be to be a productive citizen and to contribute creatively, I suppose. Kristy and I grew up in a great time, on a great street even, called Sturtevant Street. And she there, over there, Mrs. Anderson, was a real hero and teacher to many of us. She saw us grow up and seek our dreams. But something is happening or has happened. Do you want to know what that is, my story? You want to know where I've been, Mrs. Anderson?"

Lord Goodness, he turned to me, he read me, knowing I had always wondered where he'd gone. Maybe Stephen said something to him, maybe one of you kids had said something. We were all enraptured for the moment, like being caught in a spellbinding yet frightening church service, feeling drawn in and somehow being dragged in against our will by some force we were made to believe was our authority. After ten minutes or more of Cedric speaking, I wondered why no one ran or screamed more. I guess everybody figured I, the "old woman", knew him personally, and that was a safeguard.

Nothing happened. Nothing. Everyone just sat enraptured by this man, this man from Sturtevant Street I never knew would snap like this, or so it seemed back then. Our lives, our beings were changed and challenged that night.

You could feel it! I think beyond this man's troubled soul, we perceived something that rang out, something that stood convicted and confirmed.

Cedric continued. He lowered his arm and placed the gun in his jacket pocket. His teacher's posture then emerged.

"If I could simply at the end of the day say that I had shown my students examples of greatness, if I could show how great people had shared their gifts and moved someone, affected, changed, inspired society, and how they might use that as an example of their own potential gifting in the world, I would be really satisfied I had done something meaningful. For me, that is like striking gold."

Professor Miles interrupted, almost apologetically, as if to register his doubts about his own work. He said this as if he himself was counted out and was here to convince the rest of us of this, too.

"Our good brother, we are all with you. That's why we are here tonight: it's about raising consciousness, hitting the streets to win back our young people, getting in touch with just some of the things you are getting at—"

Cedric cut him off forcefully, retaking control of the audience's attention, asserting that he was going to put in his two cents without any intrusions. "Asking just those questions professor, that's why I'm here, that's why I came here tonight, that's what drives me from within, that's what keeps me sane. I'm trying to sort through all the madness and noise out there to hear clearly again. I need to remember where I came from, what my soil is. My sadness is that I don't think I will find it because the ground has gotten crusty, hardened. So you still trod your path searching for your truth. I know, "Sane?" you say, "You're not sane." Let me tell what sanity is. It's really about how you find yourself swirling in the storm, then you grab onto your questions like a floating piece of driftwood and you ask yourself for the answer out loud, then you answer back to yourself. That's sanity and that's what I seek: the freedom to ask myself the questions and having the sheer delight in hearing the answer that comes back to anchor me in the storm, because, really nobody else understands. You can't see in the storm, too much stuff flying, much of it is what somebody else is throwing at you all the time. Whether it's young people discovering themselves in time or you being here, really it's all about finding the stable moments in the storms, your identity, isn't it? Isn't it, Mrs. Anderson?

"And your questions young man, about whether it is a "Black" thing or a "White" thing?" He stepped towards Jeremy, who had posed the question.

"It's a thing thing, isn't it? How about dismantling America's greediness, selfishness, to question its resonances and to be suspicious of its shine till we find all of us glowing in discovery? I don't find this problematic at all. Why not do it yourself? Why don't we all have a moment to deconstruct? That's hearing that stability in your own storm and that is really universal to everyone."

People in the audience actually began to nod in agreement. Cedric had already long dropped the gun pointed at his head. By then his words, the things that were being shared, dispelled any fears or doubts, so no one moved away, not yet.

We were all stunned, silent, compelled to ponder his questions and still asking ourselves what this moment of madness meant—where was it going? As odd and crazed as Cedric seemed, many of the students were really hearing what he was saying. In his most pressing way, he never gave into anybody there, not even the young people by whom he seemed very much empowered. Despite his awkwardness, he was winning us all over every time he opened his mouth.

The discussion went on for well over an hour.

How we could forget that this man had been holding a gun to his head is the most amazing thing! If you can imagine nearly one hundred people gathered in an auditorium, making an inner circle, connected, communicating, no one moving away but only closer in, transfixed by this central character, that's what that night was. Our caring was the caretaker of this conversation. I cared more for us and this seemingly lost-but-being-found man so much at that moment that all else seemed to disappear. Cedric spoke so passionately—so desperate, seemingly making one last attempt to make a case for what he believed in—that alone lifted his words to a tone of meaning so that no one questioned his convictions, nor his intentions.

There was a pause in Cedric's discourse, and all the young people were standing and cheering. I noticed Cedric's eyes were closed and he was breathing in deeply, as if he were bathing in the spray of all this back-and-forth. I could see that Cedric was changing and we were changing all at once, or maybe not changing, but just resonating for this wonderful moment. I was still hyper-aware of the gun in Cedric's pocket, though—had everyone else forgotten about it?

Cedric spoke up again, his voice and spirit exhausted, his words and our words seemingly growing from his longing insides, his tormented soul. Everybody fell completely silent, and I was completely stunned into agreement. Who could argue, what could we say? We'd done it all from chaos to love and still had some lessons to take home in our back pockets, but I couldn't bear it any longer. I lost it. The discussion had been great, the young people responding, the community engaged in something we all contributed to, but no one had, as if it weren't there any more, dealt with the gun, the gun he had been holding to his head then slipped into his pocket. I addressed it. I rushed up to the mic.

"Cedric, it's been so many years, sweetheart, good to see you—but why would you want to hurt yourself or anybody like this? What did you think you were doing here this evening, scaring all these young people?"

Cedric moved to respond as the audience sucked in a collective breath, as if they'd just now remembered that this crazy lunatic had indeed been holding a gun a little while ago.

"Oh, you mean this gun, this, this pointing?" He pulled the gun from his pocket, waving it around carelessly before tossing up onto the stage. There were screams again, almost as if marking the moment's ending, as if we were all broken out of the beautiful into the harsh, frightening reality. President Summers ran to get it, but then in a humorous and relieved exclamation, proclaimed, "It's—it's plastic!"

"There was never any threat in my mind with the gun. It was just a device to hold your critical attention." Cedric stood higher on the auditorium platform.

"Fascinating, isn't it, that this is what gets us—just look anywhere today. Society has reverted to this cowboy "go get 'em, round 'em up" mentality. Presidents, politicians, pollsters, pundits, police, pimps, preachers: they are all using devices to keep our attention, aren't they? And, sadly, we listen and live by their rude routines and rhetoric. Every bit of this world's madness is a loaded gun or, hell, missile, pointed directly at our hearts and our heads. And I wish they weren't threatening, and their weapons were plastic too, but it's real and dangerous, their games. There is a danger that simmers hotter and closer to burning us each day, but young people—" Tears began to stream down his face. "It's *you* that have the choice, and the mic. Don't pull the trigger on the gun, throw it away. Reach deeper within and be the better human soul and replace those tactics of terror and the politics of empty rhetoric with the reasoning that compels us to be a better people. I know I'm not the only one who feels and thinks this way, right?"

The entire audience shouted "Yes!" back. "Right, right?" They grew louder. He continued, still sobbing through his passionate pleas.

"Asking ourselves these questions in the swirl of our storms, listening hard to the answers that come back, sorting them out, it's difficult but you have to stop and listen, then move appropriately."

He stepped off the stage, dropping down into a nearby seat, and began to weep with his face in his hands.

Dr. Strong chose that moment to hurriedly step back in, suppressing her own panic and grabbing the mic in an attempt to quiet the growing chaos within the crowd.

"Um, well, I think that really pulls so many of these pieces together. The popular culture questions, the responsibility of the cultural mechanism to project ideas, and more importantly, the critical outlook, the questions we all need to ask before we jump in, and how this prepares us to demand a better society and community. That's what we had hoped for in discussion."

She turned to her colleagues, who by this time were wiping their foreheads, gulping water down. At the end of this sharing, people were giving high fives, some rushing over to console Cedric, some talking across the entire auditorium. Students were taking notes; there was this buzz, perhaps more than what the planners envisioned. I had begun again to believe, to rise in this instance above all the anxiety I was feeling about this poor man, seemingly wrecked in mental and emotional states. In all that was being shared, I couldn't help feeling that the human capacity to love, that love removed from physical embodiment, that being, spirit and our capacity to imagine, to dream, to hope are the most powerful forcers we encounter. In some small way, Cedric was your "inner voice" that night. He had been listening from within for a long, long time, and it just exploded inside him. I heard his voice for the first time in years, and it marked my days. This joy soon turned to so many questions, though.

The police burst through the door, late as usual. What did they think they were going to do at that point? They rushed the stage; apparently someone had in fact gotten out and called them, saying "there was a maniac holding an auditorium full of students hostage with a gun." In the hurry of things, no questions were asked; they just saw all the people and misread our joy as confusion and chaos, and in that, somewhere, was danger. They arrested Cedric and hauled him away—the handcuffs, the dogs, goodness, goodness, Lord, Lord, it was some scene."

A Letter From Cedric

That was me doing my thing, causing trouble. Mrs. Anderson told those kids the tale that immortalizes my crazed actions that night. I've been spending the rest of my days running from that evening, still seeking truth. Mrs. Anderson put a heart to the tale and cooled the suspicion that I meant to hurt anyone that night. It was me that was being hurt, deeper.

Dear Mrs. Anderson,

    It's me, Cedric. I am sorry. I am so, so sorry. I know I let you down that night. I let everyone down. I am a failure and perhaps a coward, too. I am sitting here in some piss-ridden rotten motel room in a city I won't even name. I remembered your address on Sturtevant Street from all those years ago. Those were great days, Mrs. Anderson. I can still feel my feet burn from running quickly across the summer sun-baked black asphalt. I remember all the dodgeball games in the street we'd play, even after you chased us off your neighbor's lawns. Of course we'd never run across your lawn, that would have been sacrilege! You kept it like a cemetery forest or something. The smells of wet freshly mowed grass, dandelions, squished grasshoppers, and roasting marshmallows. Those colored rocks from the decorated flower beds, those arching trees, and the feeling we had that we were never going to be left alone, because everyone was watching lovingly. I need those memories these days just to keep me at least partially sane. I used to be fond of saying that I was made perfect, but in the process of living have come to be quite broken and cracked up.

So life I think, partly anyway, is about living to piece back together our brokenness. Well, today I have all my most precious belongings wrapped up in a sheet: my bible, my copy of Harold Cruse's *The Crisis*, my songs, and my coffee cups. Nobody here knows my name or my game, but I do have my music with me. I am a sad case, but I love you, Mrs. Anderson. You have always been there for me. I know it and I have always known it. Mom and Dad smile on you. That night I saw you there listening, seeing all the kids, watching that Professor Miles Brown with a proud eye and heart. Did you want me to be him? I think he's just alright. I remember him back then—he couldn't keep a beat or a lick with me and Stephen! Education and acceptance have ruined his seasoning. He makes too much sense, he needs some edge. He needs more pain in his life. Like my pain. How can he ever know what to give those kids but the books he reads and the lost dreams he can only dream of losing because he's found all the answers swimming only in his head? Anyway, I'm OK now.

They let me go, you know. I was sure you found out. The president came down in the pig's car and bailed me out. He gave the police officers all the assurances that the students that night were more moved than afraid and the exchanges allowed them to, perhaps buffer any anxieties that they may have had about the weird man. "Mr. Weirdo Cedric" was not going to come to their dorm rooms that night and shoot them or something. Anyway, as soon as they released, me I hit the road again. Usually as I leave town, I have a plan. This time, I didn't have any idea where I was going to drive or bus to next. That night I drove all night in the rain. Every drop that hit my windshield, bouncing off then another hundred replacing it made me think of myself trying to connect to something seemingly in my path, yet being pushed away by one hundred others coming behind me. I never landed anywhere Mrs. Anderson. They never let me be a part of their consistent patter. I know, you heard me say all this that night, but I don't understand the world anymore. It evades me. People disappoint me. They wear their blindness like a sight they have that allows them to have eyes in some new alien world that I am definitely not even given a sight cane to walk with in. In the eighties, after we all finished college, I think I got washed out to sea with no paddles to fend off all the bullshit that was going down. Excuse me, Mrs. Anderson. People like Miles Brown and my beloved Kristy Kilson floated towards the artificial buoys they threw out there to allow a few of us to float, but by the time I reached the shore in the nineties, I was shocked by all the broken shells left along the beach. I spent those years trying to gather up a few beach bums like me, a lover or two to join me in my various crusades for meaning. And these last years well, they ain't been no crystal stairway to heaven, or even a gangster's paradise! Since then I have been drifting on dry land with no feet, no hope, no more songs and just dry dreams. So I landed up that night, Mrs. Anderson, trying desperately to find someone to listen. I found a class, but it didn't really belong to me. So I'm on the road to nowhere again. You gave us your all. My poor parents hoped in me, but I never crystallized to any solid-made product of the dream age. I never figured out how to take all your nourishment from the root, through the stems, to allow them to blossom and flower.

You know I always believed in these crazy things, Mrs. Anderson! I believe in my music and I don't care if there's more to life than music for everybody else. I see this as the special air that if cut off, we all die. It's the sounding of a thousand connected souls trying to find home. You can hear it in every sax solo, every church moan, and every beat. That sound, feeling, is a deep history, a beautiful past and a resonating resilient future. They don't want our young people to find their home anymore. They are trying to stop the inner beats. They don't want us to hear the sound of those melodies anymore. They all make me crazy. I won't stop, Mrs. Anderson, until we have a band that plays the sounds that allow people to find their souls again. I won't stop leaving a song on every piano bench for someone to find and play, a song that allows them to discover a little catch of a tune that transforms them.

I feel like the world has decided that it would close the door on me. I don't know where I went wrong. I never pounded on the door to say, " Let me in, let me in!" I said to myself, "Maybe I can create my *own* door and I won't close it on anyone. I'll invite them all in." And everywhere I go I make that door. I polish it. I pick custom hinges so that it swings softly. I fit the door with the right handle so the doorknob fits everyone's hands. I cut a window in the door wide enough so all can see coming and going on both sides of the door. Then here they come. They smash the door, they kick it in, they trample over the host, and they say, "Hey, how do we get into the next room?" "The next room?" I say, "How about this entrance, this room I made for us to sit in? Don't you even have time to sit here a moment and be?" Nobody wants to be a real person. They all want to be a "somebody." They are all rushing to become somebodies but they never stop to be themselves. I created rooms where we could all sit and listen to some music together. You can feel a warm, sweet drink brewing in this room, and you can hear laughter in the background—not crazy laughter, but warm, light-hearted, connecting laughter, the laughter you hear when you know people care about hearing and being with each other. It's a comfortable, loving room to be in, Mrs. Anderson. And that music, we all wrote it. It sounds so good in the background, but it rings so that it's not really background music. It's the music that takes you over from the inside when you hear it because, well, somebody created it who knew what you were hoping to find in that room. It sounds like Minnie Riperton. That's the door, the room, the friends, and the music I always thought I was supposed to make in my life.

Nobody told me, Mrs. Anderson, that the key was going to modulate to human cacophony. No, don't feel sorry for me. I'm not sorry, I'm just sounding that way.

The costs of this Blues sound is a thousand wailing mothers who lost a child and a thousand crying fathers whose son never came home. That's what this music is primarily about. I have lost my reasons now for pressing onward, can't find my downbeat anymore. What am I supposed to do now? I sit here a thousand miles from nowhere, writing you a letter that will be sent from a room with no address written by a sad soul whose pen has all of a sudden run dry.

I love you, Mrs. Anderson, I always have.

Always my best,
Cedric

The Musicians

When a person dies, it is a great loss to humanity. But when an artist dies, the arts community loses a sibling, and the loss resonates in the cosmos. The stars cry, the planets mourn.

Signed, Me

I would write this on the bathroom walls at our grade school and draw a picture of a guitar, a planet, and a smiley face next to it. Nobody knew who it was, but you know now. It was me. Even then, we all believed in a world that made sense because we totally abandoned ourselves to our music. What we came out of and what I remember the older folks giving to us made us want different things. "You're gonna be somebody, turn this world upside down and out. You're gonna do it." So I took that to mean *go out and do it*.

Now, if I had to start anywhere to try and understand how all this shaped us, it would be with the musicians when we were growing up. "The people are lifted," Mrs. Anderson would say to us. "There's something about what a musician does when they do their music." She seemed, like destiny, to tell us in particular what we were supposed to do. She loved music too, even though she was not a musician. "The artists I have known over the years, troubled, yes, but sprouting on the surface as a flower singularly attached to some deep root of a creator's spirit to show us all what joy or courage or peace, power, rage and love mean." For her it was always this deeper picture. "We are always invited by them to the feast through the whisper of a song, or a boogie or the mix of a few colors angled interestingly. Do we ever really know them, as they hide to protect themselves in their own within?"

Anyway, us kids on Sturtevant Street, our parents had us into all sorts of things, from church and after school programs to foreign student exchange trips, selling soap and cleaning products, sports, young entrepreneurs, the whole bit. But in those days all the kids were into music just as excitedly as the music was memorable. As a child I had seen Jimi Hendrix on TV, a rock'n'roll star who looked like me. He was doing something extraordinary with his guitar, something totally original his own way, and I remember thinking, "That's something for me." He was making music, his music, his way. So my mother, and then later my father, nurtured that.

On my block, there was me, Stephen Lucas, and the rest of the gang. Stephen and I were really melded together from the very beginning. Stephen was a PK, a preacher's kid. He was the captain of the local neighborhood Birney Elementary safety patrol and I was his first lieutenant. Our posts spanned the Russell Woods neighborhood down several blocks, in front of the school, and past Birney to the "hoods" where the "bad kids" and their families lived. No fences, just "nice" grass and "bad tore up ghetto grass" as they called it, separated these neighborhoods. "Got to get them safely across and over Broadstreet through the hood and to school, all before 7:30 am. That way we can get to the hot cocoa and oatmeal, man," Stephen would tell me on those cold Michigan winter mornings during our daily routine. I've often wondered if that was a code for a lesson in life, getting the people safely across the broad-streets as if we were to deliver as duty. Or maybe life was to be lived waiting for the cushioned moments that sweet, creamy, steamy broth brought as it mustached you and protected from the cold we had to face everyday.

We were the young musicians too, playing in school bands, church camp bands, after school bands and talent shows; this is how we bonded and entered that special sect that ultimately protected us. Bands are the ultimate communal channel for musicians. Stephen and I likened ourselves to a dynamic duo like Jimi Hendrix and Larry Graham, playing guitar and electric bass and ruling the world. These were the days when you would listen to the radio, tape-record the songs, and then learn them from what was called "taking it off the record." Everybody had to learn their own individual parts in those days, and then bring it all together to play. That's how you made music.

Stephen was always getting in trouble with his parents because there was a conflict of interests. Stephen's father was the pastor of a prominent traditional Baptist church, and that was a big deal in Detroit. Stephen was supposed to be helping his mom, brothers, and sisters doing the music for the services, not rehearsing with neighborhood band mates. Sunday morning, worship. Monday night, choir rehearsal. Tuesday night, auxiliary and church group meetings. Wednesday night, bible study. Thursday night, young ministries fellowship. Friday night and Saturday night too. There was always something or other, then back again to Sunday. We never thought of this as much of a problem, this was just the way church families lived. It was their family business.

I always seemed to be a bad influence on Stephen because I was into pop, rock, and R&B. His mother would lament, "You know, that Cedric is rooted in confusion, Stephen. I'm praying for that young man." My parents had me selling soap products, "developing business and people skills that you need in this world," as my mother would repeatedly tell me. I was into camps, youth foreign exchange programs, but I did talent shows at church and I loved roller skating. The music blasted you 'round the rink! I'm sure this was a den of hell to the Lucases. Stephen seemed always torn between wanting to grow up to be a musician and being shaped to be a preacher and directing his mother's church choirs. This was kind of symptomatic of traditional Black identity, though—"torn asunder," as Dubois wrote, fighting within one's insides to keep it all together. Black people's culture is always in a fight for values from within the community and against an American backdrop which has always been ambiguous and out of balance. That hasn't changed much. W.C. Handy, the Father of the Blues, his father was a minister too. He swore he'd rather see his son dead than see him as a musician, chasing the devil's music. But the music wasn't the devil's, it was his son's.

Black people had to do something respectable for their people, and we've always had our music. For us and everybody around there was lots of music. Why, they had pop music on AM radio, gospel, R&B, rock'n'roll, and jazz, and it all seemed to flow back and forth. We had access to it all because somebody played it on the radio. The DJ's on those local radio shows should be recognized as the public music teachers for the community. Their choices, comments, and love for what the music was about was amazing.

The Radio blasted DJ Donny Sounds Simpson's voice, that smooth confidence that you depended on to keep you in the right groove. And everybody was on it, heads bobbing, everybody singing cooly and sweetly even as the summer heat roasted the dashboards' small radio speakers, lost in the thump of those beats and songs.

As a musician you could dream, fuss with all the styles. None of this, though, was like kids running away to find themselves by dressing in black or piercing their bodies, spiking, bleaching hair and then cutting themselves for attention. For us, the music was about *the music*, the sounds, about grooving together, making something amazing. Anyway, as kids we practiced and played and played, and like rival gangs, we had rival bands that would play after school for the neighborhood parties, talent shows sponsored by the different schools, and community houses.

Stephen would say, "Hey, Cedric, *girls*, man, they might give you some if you play right, something they can groove on. They *love* musicians." From the beginning I never had problems attracting the girls—it was them sticking around long that grew to be the problem. Anyway…

On Sturtevant Street, there was one boy, Bobby Watson, whose dad was a "businessman." Mr. Watson was one of those fancy Black industries kind of fellows in the community, with a big new Cadillac seemed like every year. He was fashioned and diamond down with cane, hat, always in and out, and always busy, with "business" kinds of things. "Businessman, businessman, doing your thang," the neighbors would say and wave from across the street. That was a code for "suspect." Bobby, who wasn't very talented, came up with his contribution to our art. We on the block had formed a band and were playing these local talent shows, even a few radio shows. We were really starting to get some recognition. But with a band you need equipment, and, while parents supplied the basics, the new what they called "effects"—wah-wah pedals, new cords, new amplifiers—were the kinds of items that average parents didn't have the money for in those days. No toys, just the basics.

"What are your father and I doing spending our hard-earned, just so you can feel fancy?" Mom would say. "Ohhh, no! Make your music first with all these lessons we pay for and forget about fancy." So you had to have paper routes at that age to keep up with the musical needs. Bobby came up with a plan. He called it "his contribution." Since he knew that his father's business created several "departments of finance," those monies came into the house regularly and were stashed safely at home. Bobby knew where his dad stashed all the loose "departments loot." His plan was to stage a break-in after school. He was mastermind. He went onto become some leading executive-type later, of course. He came home, took his dad's stash, broke out of a back window, climbed down, and then later pretended to come home, finding broken windows and calling the police. It worked. Police reports were made, our story well concocted. After things simmered down a bit, Bobby and band had cash in hand.

Nobody took a cab in those days, especially all the way downtown. It just would cost too much. But on this band buying day, all us kid musicians hopped in the cab, dashed downtown to Grinnell's and bought hundreds of dollars of new cords, wah-wah pedals, drums, the whole bit. I never saw money spent like that before, so I closed my eyes, squinted, and just pointed at goods. Well, we being good church boys swore we hadn't done anything but accepted the "toys." The band found ourselves in an awkward discordant dilemma.

Sure enough, it didn't take many days for the parents to become suspicious of all the new sounds, glitter, and more consistent regular rehearsals. Somebody leaked it. My mom followed me into the basement one day after school. "Cedric, where did you boys get all this stuff from, all this equipment? Where did all this come from, Cedric?"

"We needed it for the gigs mom."

"I didn't ask you what you needed it for, son! Your father and I asked where it came from, and where did you all get the money for all this stuff you have been using?"

She didn't buy my unconvincing response about savings from newspaper routes, or talent shows, or the like, and neither did any of the other parents. The moms called a meeting and the band was sequestered to the Sturtevant "high court." Mrs. Pitts was a neighbor, a mother of a band member, and she worked for the county judge. She presided. She was as sharp as a prosecuting attorney. She made each of us tell where and how the band got all this new equipment. She was tough.

"Boys, this is no joke. We are all saddened by this family theft. You all should be ashamed!"

We all said as if it were a choir cue, "We're sorry, we didn't know—it was for—"

"It was for what?" She charged back. We just thought they'd all really appreciate what we could do with our band with all that great equipment.

"Everything we play now sounds..." as we said to them, "Amazing. But we didn't steal anything."

We all sounded so sure this could make a difference in the minds of the judge and the very pissed-off parents sitting and hearing this as the jury.

"We just used Bobby's dad's money. He said his dad wouldn't miss it anyway. We were doing good with the money to make the band better."

Right! But the parents didn't see our "investment" as anything the least bit appreciable or wholesome. Bobby was not invited to this. He had to deal with his own parents, who were not pleased either. We all came clean at once. "It was his plan, he said it would be alright."

"Alright?! Oh really, you thought this would be alright?. Did you all even think about what your friend was doing taking from his own parents? Or that maybe this would have all backfired and Bobby could have fallen, or been injured with this crazy scheme?" All the ambition, promise and feeling of good intention for the sake of the betterment of our band evaporated into nothingness. I began to get really nervous, scared at the frightful prospects of breaking the law.

"The way it was thought about was that the money would never be missed, because it was "extra money," we guessed. We just thought it would help all of us and never thought it would hurt anyone, but we know now that this was a huge mistake."

"Huge mistake! You better believe it, and we as your parents are not going to let any of you off the hook for such a mistake that all of us have to bear and deal with now."

Mrs. Pitts, now more heated and legally in the mindset, took great strides and went into scary detail to remind us that these were actual crimes. She never let up for a minute. We were in deep, deep doo-doo and feeling the strain of what the old people called "keeping blues close" quite heavily. After some talking and comparing notes with the other parents, Judge Pitts made the final pronouncement. We waited, completely freaked out. There was a lot here on the line: punishment, allowances cut, no TV, those stinging belt spankings from anxious and ready dads to whoop some behinds, perhaps even jail? Lastly, and most devastatingly, the future of our band hung in the balance.

"We have decided you will all be grounded, and the band will be permanently dis-banded. We have been working on some alternative summer plans for you all in terms of some neighborhood projects to keep you busy." It was through Mrs. Pitts "court" and our parents cooperation that the band scam was found out, and corrected again permanently. Mr. Watson was silent throughout this, and luckily Bobby's parents didn't press charges against their son nor us, which was a godsend. It was really breaking and entering with intent.

We never saw too much of Bobby after that. His parents sent him away to a boarding school. The band had to give all the equipment back to the store, the money returned to the Watsons, and that was, of course, the end of the funk for that funk band! To this day, for thirty years I've been running around in an attempt to get my band reformed.

You know, I never believed that village theory about raising children was something that came from Africa. No, that wasn't from

Africa, that was from Sturtevant Street. They believed in keeping the kids together and on watch. We didn't need any police officers, social workers, because the policemen and the social workers were the neighbors on the block. Every household kept watch. That's the way it was. By Stephen and my parents pulling us out of the neighborhood band, it forced us to play with the kids at school from then on. We met new musicians, but the home band was the real deal that grounded us. It was our faith.

"You see son, I told you about the devil's music and his ways." Stephen's folks didn't miss the beat on this one. Now mind you, this was the kind of correction "bad kids" in Russell Woods went through. Somehow the parents believed that they had to be purposeful about what company and activities we all kept, but still the music grew even deeper within us and we came to live in it.

The music that streamed from cars, radios, basements in the pop culture of the day was the most beautiful thing for everybody. The day James Brown died, Christmas Day 2006, was a horrible Christmas gift for Black America. His very presence made us all tall, no matter what. James Brown was inspiration and a beacon of hope for us. He was somebody who performed a music that went along with Black people defining themselves as a people in society. The music represented what freedom and living with dignity meant and promised for us in America. "Say It Loud, I'm Black and I'm Proud," that's about living in a society, in an America that formerly defined us as bound, non-existent and of no hope. I think his music, and what he believed it was doing, released in us a dance, a step, a sound, spirit, a feeling that set us free, really: *Say it loud, I'm Black and I'm proud*. And being Black, and being proud, meant something. Mrs. Anderson's, my mother's generation had swing and Louis Jordan, but they never moved to the point of social consciousness that was like ours. That's what we had going on around us and inside of us as kids on Sturtevant Street.

Before Mrs. Anderson took over as principal at the high school, she was a literature and civics teacher in primary, then middle school. Mrs. Anderson got her masters in the mid-fifties from Wayne State University in Detroit when most everyday Black people couldn't even sit at the counter at local drugstores to have a cup of coffee. "We had to be ready to take our places, or live with the prospects of remaining slighted. We just couldn't live with that." She really, really wanted to teach in the school system. Her husband died early and they never had children of their own, so she took to giving her all to every kid she came into contact with, and when she came home after school she had a street full of more young people who looked up to her. As a neighbor on Sturtevant Street, she took care to watch out over all of us. Mrs. Anderson was my second truth, another mother, and she was dedicated to teaching young people. In her classes, she made all the kids write poems about popular music and dancing and all. Even then, all the teachers thought she was crazy. "She's wasting her time with that popular trash. It's just not serious material," she'd tell us of their whispering among the teachers in those days.

She played the popular not-classical music in the class and got her students singing and dressing up. The classes emulated the great singers and musicians of the day. Diana Ross and The Supremes, they were real lady-like on TV. The girls sang "Please Mr. Postman" or the guys did The Temptations' "Beauty's Only Skin Deep." She also used to have them copy the song words, sing them, but you had to tell a story about what they meant to you. This was a marvelous thing, because it taught us that the songs all said something.

We believed the world we were going to be a part of would change. You could feel this, and as a teacher naturally she encouraged us. Again, the most focused picture you got from those songs was that we were beautiful and our lives were valuable. They say the soundtrack to your life is the music you grew up on. The Sturtevant Street kids grew up in a music that was not only a soundtrack, it was the continuous sound bite and the soul-connecting source for who we were. Our weekend basement parties held a fascinating connection with us growing up, and growing into the world we kids were to be a part of. I still remember what the times felt like because I remember the music pumping loud, the way the music made you feel. There were all these things that seem so normal, so the way it was, that it stamped some essential values, sayings, beliefs that wrapped you up in the blends of the rhythms and the songs.

The sixties-seventies Sturtevant Street kids had all that. Our music had to be a full flowering of all we hoped and lived for. That music soul-stuff was enough to set the world on fire. And it did. I was deeply cemented within the idea of setting things on fire. You following?

Dad and Mom's Stories

"Bring a child up in the ways of the Lord, oh yes, and they shall never depart from it. So plan your work and work your plan, stay on it and don't depart from it till the job is done."

My mother was very sure of her sayings. "That's what I always tell you, son, right?" She had this way of saying and mixing up old schoolmarmish bible verses and business philosophy lines she gained over the years. These run through me now like melodies looking to unlock and resolve all my dissonances unresolved.

My mom and dad were around Mrs. Anderson's age. They gave me a fantastic upbringing. I miss my parents. They were my dear friends.

I was an only child, so you can imagine that the kids on Sturtevant Street really were brothers and sisters to me. As I was growing up, besides Stephen, there was only my one cousin, Devonne Divine. She is a mad woman. Can you believe someone would name a child that? She is precious, though, a real story, that child.

I remember how my parents and the old folks used to sit in the backyard and tell all us kids, and all who would gather at our house, stories about living in the Depression. We were there seated on lawn chairs, some seated Indian style, some sprawled out on the grass, the hot summer sun directly above us. It hovered there, and it listened too.

"You see, we children of the Depression were, in some ways, in a better place than your group because we already didn't have anything, so we held onto and appreciated the little things like self-pride and dreaming about becoming and doing all you could so nobody could tell you you couldn't be the best." I loved hearing those stories, as did the other kids, who asked what it was like and how people dressed?

These were the Bar-B-Q summers. Everybody cooked. You could smell those special sauces from backyard to backyard. Stevie Wonder was playing on the radio. Kids played skip rope. Usually the boys were in the backyard playing basketball. The older folks were always seated under the shade umbrellas with lemonades in hand, watching, talking, and swatting flies. It was summer, so there were always a few young couples that were getting married.

On this one day in June, my parents were celebrating their 30th wedding anniversary. They redid their vows and had a wonderful party in our backyard. That day, they told the best stories, which were about their early days of marriage and our family history. That fascinated everybody there, young and old, neighbors and family. "Alright, Mrs. Sullivan," someone asked, "what was it like coming up in school and then getting married and all, thirty years ago?"

My mom, in her floppy hat, shorts, and soft summer top, began almost falling into a warm trance, her story pulling us all into some kind of vortex of welcomed memories. She began.

"Well, Cedric's dad and I were married after he returned from the service in 1946. We had a glorious wedding! My husband's best friend Jessie Harvell was the best man. He was a great musician who was in the music department at Cass Tech High. Although he never took it seriously, he was very gifted, but he never pursued it to anything. Essie Ross was my maid of honor. We were great reading partners. They would have these reading rooms in the public library where they let Black people come in and read. We were both very fond of just reading and sitting with each other and spent much of our time that way.

"Anyway, Bill and I had our honeymoon in the upper Peninsula of Michigan at St. Ignace. It was unheard of in those days for most young Black couples, and for a whole lot of white people, to have honeymoons. Our family thought we were crazy! We made the seven hour drive in his 1939 Theroplane. Bill stuffed 6 fully blown-up tires and a couple of gas cans in the back seat and we were off!

"In those days, I worked for a Black lawyer who actually owned a hotel there and encouraged us to go up. We stayed in his hotel, which was for Blacks.

"This was all right after Bill got out of the war. I made sure that if I was going to wait for him, he'd be walking up that aisle soon as he got out! Well, during War World II and through all the 1940's, finding employment was very difficult. During the high school years, they put you in a certain group, general groups, like home economics. The teachers put me in the home economics curriculum, which taught sewing, cooking, and cleaning. My mother would not have it, so she went over there and told the teachers, "I want my daughter to be educated to be more. I can teach her to sew, cook, and clean at home; you folks teach her something useful here."

"My mother was from High Shoals, Georgia, born about 1900. This was shortly after slavery, and things were changing. You see, years ago, Spellman College was like a little one room high school. If a kid was smart enough and finished that school, they would get a certificate and probably went on to become a teacher at the same school or another Black school. All those Black colleges started out like that. My mother was smart enough and more, so she taught at Spellman. That's where my mama came from, that's where she learned to stand up for herself, so she had no problem marching right up to my school and telling them to take me out of home economics.

"At that time, my skills were high, but that didn't make any difference because I was Black. But thanks to my mother's insistence, I could type and do shorthand at the same speed as my teachers when I was in the 10th grade, so they put me in the high school office. It was Edna Volks, the principal, who put me into the office, in the front. After high school I went to Wayne State University with a double curriculum in business. I wanted to go into court recording, but they wouldn't let Black people do that.

"It was terrible in the North, because it was geared to putting through the white kids and holding you back. I remember when I applied for a job at the Michigan Bell Telephone Co. They were bringing in all these hillbilly girls who couldn't even speak the King's English! They told me they wouldn't put me in there because I had an *accent*. So I decided to go into the service-oriented group in the core. I went on an interview at the mustering-out point for the troops to be a stenographer. I had to go way up to Battle Creek, Michigan. I was the only Black girl on that bus, but I made friends with a white girl. Her daddy was the President of the First Bank and Trust of Michigan. She just wanted to get with the soldiers. When we arrived to take the skills test, do you know every white girl on that bus passed, but I didn't? My friend walked right up to the man running the test and said, "You are a goddamn lie! Anna here types at 65 words a minute. I can't type, I don't know shorthand, I don't have those skills, and I passed, so how could this happen?" You know, there are some good white people in this world and we can attest to that. That girl threatened, "I am going to tell my daddy." The commander called her father, and by the time I got back home, they had called my mother and told her that they had made a mistake, and that I needed to report to the Federal building in downtown Detroit on Monday morning. That very afternoon I had a job at the city core as a stenographer for the government. They would not assign me to an officer as a secretary, though, so they initiated a steno pool, that is, those that take the over load of work. So I was busy all the time making money, developing my skills, waiting on my husband to come home from the War.

"Anyway, I was the only Black girl in this secretarial pool. They had two other girls who were elevator operators, but when they went on break, they made *me* operate the elevator! So, again, my mother intervened. "My daughter was brought here as a secretary, not an elevator operator. She will *not* operate an elevator!" For a Black woman to tell a white man in those days what to do was something! Captain Van Dam wasn't going to put down my mother, so he put me back in the office. I developed my skills so much that I was able to work for lawyers in the court downtown soon after.

"I worked for two lawyers, Julian Rodgers and Julian Perry. Julian Rodgers was high class, from the West side, but Julian Perry could pass for white. He would get all the clients. The judges would give him the different cases over Attorney Rodgers. Rodgers had to work as a bus driver at night in order to take care of his family. I serviced all their clients by taking the bill of complaints. I took them to the federal building. What I was actually doing was building my own business. I started a secretarial service, doing my thing because I knew I had to have more than one skill to survive in this white man's world. Mr. Perry would get drunk. He became depressed. He couldn't present his cases. So I would have to go up to the judge and say, "Oh, judge, Attorney Perry is sick today, he can't present the cases, so I'd like a stay of appointment for these clients." So the judge, Judge Volks, who knew me through his sister, my principal in high school, said, "Young lady, you are a liar. I saw Attorney Perry drunker than a dizzy fool when I got out of my car this morning! Young lady, you can do this job. You are actually the lawyer for both of these men. You better get back in school." At that time they weren't allowing Black women to do much of anything, but he saw something in me and encouraged me."

My dad interrupted her then. "He encouraged you because we had Black people around who were setting fine examples and doing things for themselves."

Of course, all the old folks break in too, like a choir on cue, "Oh, yes, oh, yes, don't you know it!" My dad went on.

"This is what bothers me! We were self sufficient. At least these guys were regulated to take care of their own! Lawyers, doctors, Black architects, Black engineers, Black business owners were abound. This was all *before* integration. Black people took care of their own. We had to do all these things and so I have to ask, "What happened to us?" It's really something. Integration was good in one way and terrible in another way. It tore us asunder. It made us less self-sufficient than we had been before. All the stores and what not, insurance companies, hotels? Hastings Street? I mean, I mean, they portray us as dumb and not doing anything, but I remember we had it together. We got the money from each other because the financial institutions were not helping the Black people. We were able to generate the money, the products for our community."

There wasn't any of us kids sitting around that day who didn't get that message of self determination from dad's rant. And all the older people said, "Mmmmm-hmmm, yes, Lord, ain't it the truth."

Mom continued with her own story.

"When I was fourteen or fifteen, Jessie Slaton was the first Black lawyer in the city. She was my role model. Jessie Slaton taught me that "Double V begins with Me." Victory begins with me. I brought that with me through my work with communities. It was a victory over poverty, to make us successful." She slowed down, raising up a small finger, pointing and shaking it as she would do to be sure we *got* it.

"My earliest recollections, though, were when my daddy worked for the railroads. This would have been about 1930. Those jobs were ten or twelve hours a day. If a Black man was found in the streets walking alone, the police would arrest him, beat him and take him to jail for being on the streets. Just beat them senseless. So my mother would get all six of us dressed at night and walk us all the way to Hastings Street and Watson. And when daddy got off of that streetcar, all of us were there, and we walked daddy home every night so they wouldn't pick him up and take him down to the station."

The real drama for us kids listening to all this was whose story was better. Mom and Dad went full at it in the exchange, further drawing us all in. My dad took his turn then, supplementing Mom's story.

"To the white people, if a Black person was out that time of night, you were up to no good. In those days, they had a group of cops who called themselves "Black Moriahs." I don't know how they came up with that name. They had these long black cars; they would round up Black guys, beat 'em all up. It happened all the time."

I loved watching them, hearing their stories. That's how I learned the history, and how I was sure I needed to share, to shape others in this way, too.

Mom looked at Dad, a little bit peeved, before going on with her own thing.

"Now, my mother taught me the basic things she brought up from the South. How to sit like a lady and cross your legs. And you know what that means? If you crossed your legs, wasn't nothing getting in there! That was the way we were taught in my generation. So by the time I was married—" My dad interrupted again. "Now that's the good part! Tell 'em, honey!"

"*Anyway*, by the time I was married, lessons like that weren't being taught as much. I was able to take a job at the Brewster Center to teach young mothers how to take care of their families, take care of themselves. At this point these mothers didn't have fathers for the children, and that was a sho' 'nuff no-no in those days. I went out to these broken families and I taught them how to plan their day. I always tell Cedric here, "Do good for good, the good doing way, with all the goods you have." I learned that early on in my life.

"During my childhood, we lived on the West side during the Depression, and many people lost their homes. I remember Erskin Street, but I remember happy family life: my daddy worked and he came home, while my mother, naturally, stayed home with the children. We did our homework at night around the table. I had a very pleasant life. We went to school, we went to church, all like a family. All the people in my family came as a group up from the South: the Graves, the Tuckers, the Thrashers all moved to Detroit together. My parents and their brothers and their sisters, who were grown, all came looking for jobs and landed in Detroit.

"When we were on Erskin street we lived in tenement houses. That's two families in each house, and we lived downstairs. Nothing separated us from the ground, so rats could gnaw themselves up into our living quarters, so they could go certain places, like closets and such. My father would save tin cans, then would flatten them out. He would put the tin down and nail it right into that spot so the rats couldn't get up in to that area. It worked, most of the time. A rat got up in my bed one night and bit me. That was such a traumatizing thing. Even with the rats, we were happy and very family-oriented. Every morning there was a pot of oatmeal on the table and then we went off to school."

Us kids listening to Mom's story yelled about the rats, disgusted and disbelieving, reduced to a yard full of squeamish youths. The older people were all laughing, my parents enjoying this immensely.

Although I realize it now, I didn't appreciate the lessons of the stories at that time. They made me uncomfortable. These stories trapped me, marked me inside, and I waited to run from all this as a kid. Why?

My dad picked up the thread with his own side of the story, weaving in and out of memories.

"Well, getting back to the way it was. I knew the beginning of "public accommodation" for Black folks when it was the new law of the land. If I can recall correctly, this happened on July 19, 1963. By this time, Cedric had been born, and we brought him down to Dallas because I had a job assignment there. I said, "This is great, I can go to any picture show I want even down here in the deep South." So one afternoon I picked the most expensive show downtown I could find, paid my two or three dollars, whatever it was, and the woman gave me my ticket and change. She didn't even think about it. The guy at the door took my ticket. The way I walked, it just took them by surprise. Nobody said anything! At that point, no Black person had been in that show before me. I integrated that show! So I went down the aisle, it was *The Nutty Professor* that was playing, and I was enjoying it. Again, this was the *very* day in 1963 that this edict from Washington had come down, so the ushers came over and said, "How did you get in here ?" I explained that I gave the cashier my money and bought a ticket. "What do you mean, she gave you a ticket?" they said. My ignorance of Southern laws helped, but I didn't know that they didn't know, but what they knew for sure was, that I wasn't from around there. "Excuse me, but this theater is not integrated, Sir. Black people can't be here." I said, "The law was just passed that allows anyone who pays and wishes to see a movie to be admitted. I thought you all knew."

"The young men looked surprised and still assured, "Well, we don't know anything about this law. So, this is the choice: we can give you your money back and you leave, or you can sit over there near the side, because we don't have any place for Black people to sit." So four of them, trying not to create a scene, took me over to the far end of the theater. Then three of them left and one stayed there and sat with me during the whole movie. Once the show was over, four or five of the young men came back over and walked me out to the sidewalk. It may have seemed like they were kicking me out, which I didn't care that much about because I had by that time sat and seen the whole movie. They took me out a side door, looked up and down the street, and then escorted me to the sidewalk. I didn't think about it then, but what they were really doing was trying to protect me. They were possibly saving my life.

"When I got home, I told my wife Anne here what had happened. She said, "Fool, don't you know they could have just taken you off the road somewhere and lynched you or something? And nobody would have known about it! Why would you do such a thing?" She was very upset. I thought that was really dumb of me but I just hadn't been aware of the danger I was in. This was July, but it was November 22 of that same year when they assassinated Kennedy. After that, I was real careful of how I carried myself down there.

"Now you all shouldn't wonder about those things so much because it wasn't but a minute ago that the tanks and armed patrols roamed our streets here in Detroit in 1967. The riots were not far from our protected Sturtevant Street, and ripped through very near here. All the neighborhoods were entangled in street violence. The National Guard was sent in to escort you kids to school. Remember that? Their job was to keep order and dissipate any of the people's upsurges, to stop the spread of the rage due to the disappointment of the Black communities after the King, Malcolm and Kennedy assassinations.

"Those tanks seemed so out of place, surreal, so robot-like. I mean, you all had your G. I. Joe with Kung Fu Grip as toys, and now here were these soldiers, live, up close, and on your blocks taking over. It seemed so un-American that our streets would be arrested or on curfew and entangled in this dispute over what was best for Black communities, and what was best for the country at large. In some ways we felt, although denied the liberty of having the run of our own communities, quite special to be in such a stream of protections, special privileges, and in the spotlight." He had hit another nerve deep within me. Who could determine what we could do? I was indignant, even at that age.

"I had been a part of the earlier Detroit riots. The 1943 riots were much more devastating. I was right there in it at 19, and I had to go to jail." My dad seemed almost entranced. "Homes and businesses got burned up and down 12th street. We heard a rumor that the police had stopped a couple unjustifiably on the Belle Isle Bridge and a fight ensued. The police threw their child in the water and this precipitated concerns in the Black community. People heard about this in the neighborhoods; the story about this policeman throwing a child off a bridge got bigger and bigger. Looting began.

"So the guardsmen had to come in and calm everything down. During the riot, I had five guys with me: Wimpy Harris, Sonnyboy Davis, Norman Johnson, Johnny B. Brownly, and his younger brother Jesse. So here we go up to Hastings street. We are walking up and see all these places busted out. We were just innocent bystanders, we hadn't actually done anything. But on the way back, fearing white folks across the railroad tracks on the way home, I decided to pick up a piece of glass and put it under my sweatshirt. As we were coming back, there came the police. The cops stopped us and they patted us down. They found this piece of glass in my pocket. "Here is a weapon! You no-good, trouble-making boys—we're taking you down to jail." I was 19, the oldest one of the bunch, so they took me in. They kept me in jail for three days! It worked out as a protection of sorts actually. By that time, it had gotten violent outside in the streets; people were shooting. Hell was going on in Detroit. Killings, burnings of buildings, so much stuff happened that I actually felt safe and protected being in the jail. I always thought of it as police protective custody. They called up my mother to come and get me out since there were no charges pressed against me. I got out, perfectly fine. This was 1943, right before I was to go into the war, June or July. I had to go in August.

"Now, my mother's boyfriend, Mr. Frank, owned a store in a white Polish neighborhood. It was on Canfield and Chene Street Station. This was the only Black-owned store in this neighborhood. They knew this and came in to destroy the store. Frank had a registered pistol and he always carried it. They broke through the door and Frank shot one of them while they dispersed. He was just a Black man protecting his store, but he killed a White man. Because of that, he was put in jail, charged with manslaughter, and served for three years. When he came out, it was just a little bit before I came out of the army in 1946.

"They pushed the draft up right after the riots to get the Black kids off the street. I showed them my credentials. I had graduated in 1942 from Cass Tech in Aeronautic Design. I was sure I'd go into the Air Force. I was working during this period at Ford Motor Company, which allowed the young people to get training at the Ford trade school. I was paid 50 cents an hour! Welding skills, machinist, internal grinder, a three-month training period, and during that time is when I got my notice. So I took it to my job supervisor to get a deferment. They said, "No, you have to report and go to the induction station." They put me in, the Quarter Master signed me up, and sent me off. I was inducted into the service. My mother was crying, my future wife was crying. I had a 1939 Theroplane at the time, so I had to find a place to put it. Frank was away in jail and my mother had to operate the store. Anne, my future wife, and I couldn't get married. It was devastating! While everyone struggled, my mother Carrie helped everyone make it through.

"Now, Cedric's grandmother here, Mama Carrie, was born in 1896. By the time I was born, she was a much older lady in her late twenties who had taken up with a guy who never stayed around. In those days folks sometimes altered the records, didn't quite tell the whole story. Anyway, my mother had all her brothers and sisters to take care of; the family was very close and everybody loved my mother. She was the one who kept the family together." My grandmother sat there listening quietly and queenly with a soft smile. I always remembered her as resting in her stored wisdom, all in there.

"Well, Uncle Bud, her eldest brother, had plenty of money. Zeke Sullivan, *my* grandfather, was born a slave. The story is that when my grandfather died, Uncle Bud Sullivan was the executor of the estate, the family's earning and all. Now Zeke had money in the bank and actually had a real good job once he arrived North after he sent his family up. He sent them all up in the 1900's. What they had to do, since they were sharecroppers and they couldn't leave, was to get the family out of the South. Prior to leaving, they made sure that some of the earnings from the pigs, corn, crops and all were hidden from the boss-man owner. In other words, they altered the books showing earnings but greater losses. They used this money to finance the leave. They made their plans to come up North, which included having these goods to take with them to make some money. Bud was the first one to leave out of there with stuff on freight cars. They shipped it, got places for them, and they all came in piecemeal. Bud's job was to find homes or places for everybody to live. As the story goes, they left in groups. Once they settled, something happened that was an unforeseen blessing: the old white landowner died and left the land to his "now not-so trusted Zeke." My grandfather decided to sell the land and was the last one to leave; he left running, too! From this one shack, all these folks prepared and planned to go North. And that's how we got up here. When I think about it, none of my people even had a high school diploma, and to go to college was unheard of. That's the way it was back then. Now when Zeke arrived, he got a job at a factory. But shortly after, he was killed on the job because something fell down off the line directly on his head.

"Edna, my grandfather Zeke's wife, passed soon after. That was the old evil "White man's revenge," as my aunts would say.

"So as the story goes, uncle Bud had parceled out the money from the insurance, the sales of stuff and it was all a part of the money that those *nine* brothers and sisters divided up and that's how the family got settled in the North. This is how we got this story, 'cause it was like the old methods of storytelling and how the old folks would pass on the family history. Of course that's all gone away now, except for Mama Carrie still here with us, but this is how I got the story."

When he finished we were all amazed.

Of all the things I treasure the most, it was those times of sharing where history walked before my eyes. All of us, even the older folks, would sit there, delightfully numbed by these vivid illustrations of real-life stories from my parents' past.

That they could envision a world, a life better for us, their children, and generations after is the kind of thing I dreamed to work for, too. None of them wanted our people to be saddled with that kind of discrimination or defeat before you even got out of the gate. By the time we'd grown up, it was the seventies, the eighties, and these were the days our generation saw the changes.

Shift in Time Out of Tune

It was in the late 1970's. I can still smell the fumes and feel the pavement tremble from the rumble of those engines revving up in front of the school.

I remember those elevators that we had to take us up to our classes. They were big industrial-like, chain-drawn elevators that fifty kids could fit into. We jammed into those elevators that seemed to "beam us up, Scotty" to our classes. Cass Tech was huge and tall. For us, it represented a view of perhaps what the corporate, business-busy world we were leaving to conquer was like. Cass Tech had the number-one high school music program around, and city kids came specifically to study music as a technical major. Wind, concert, marching, and jazz bands, orchestra, choirs, harp and vocal, harp ensemble, an all-state award-winning symphonic wind band, Cass Tech had it all. We knew music, and we lived for it there.

I took all this way too far, as Cass Tech made us believe that all was possible. The world changed fast in the 1980's. It seemed to grow into another kind of monster, and I don't think the real creative world was a part of that new era, so they really sent us into a time that was geared up for corporate success. I just wasn't shaped that way from the insides. We all left there ready to march into Reagan's "fucking reign" and the new "me reality show." I went away to college and spent my professional training time in the Northeast learning to be a musician, totally believing that my preparation was a further tuning up to meet the world with the "right song." I graduated into the eighties and that's the world in which I died and lost my soul, as well as my mind.

So now it was the early nineteen-eighty-something's. I was twenty-something years old and I landed in Los Angeles, and while the smoke of the 1960's was a distant memory to us, the lasting fumes of that social explosion of the 1970's propelled us like fuel. As musicians, we had all dreamed the dream by now of what it meant to be famous. Hip hop music hadn't moved us as musicians yet because, I mean, we were *musicians* and we weren't really a part of that movement. Ours had been a movement of music, ideas, and personalities as wide as the cosmic funk of George Clinton and as sweet as the lyrical soulfulness of Minnie Riperton, my favorite, of course. Hearing her sing was the first time I wept at the sound of a woman's voice.

These ideas stretched the meaning of funk, moving the butt and grabbing the mantle of the social ladder-makers. We were ready to make us a world, and with our eduma-cation in our back pockets, who would tell us to be silent? You look at me like I'm crazy!

That is what we saw. I'm telling you. You sit there and wonder how I came here after spending twenty years digging holes trying find my truth, huh? I'll tell you what happened! Something happened. Something happened right in there! There were traces of destruction, too, disparity and denial all the way back because somebody dropped the ball on faith, keeping it strong, pushing beyond the barriers. I'm sure my insanity, my instability has something to do with my frustration in people losing their direction, soul, soil and their faith in us. There is no future now, just a decaying present which we are now doomed to watch unravel. That's our future. Some of this is our own doing, but we partake in this foolishness conscious of our own destruction. It's a dysfunctional social pathology. We are locked into these jails of despair after centuries of horrific attacks, so these damages we play out like breathing air, normalcy. You have to adjust the conditions that perpetuate hate and oppression before the people will heal properly. Well, anyway.

You ask, what happened to Cedric? I had all the promises in my back pocket. And yeah, I certainly benefited from affirmative action—it's called my mother and father.

They taught me to work to maintain the higher elevation of my specialness, and that the world will never be able to reduce me down to just another Sam or Sally.

Like I said, we had left a decade of cultural springboards into what was hoped would be a bright social future for all. The eighties were *fresh to discover*. We had all the *Right Stuff*. The decade opened *beautifully*: John Lennon killed in New York and Marley dead the following August. *Great* start. Anyway, I took all the money I had saved from post-college drudge jobs and caught a plane to Los Angeles. I figured I could move out there after graduation, instrument and a few contacts in hand. My parents, God must love them, washed their hands of me believing I was to become my own man. They kicked me out of the warm nest and forced me to fly.

The East Coast at that time seemed so overloaded with musicians trying to find the next jazz gig, chasing the only carrot they had at the time—playing in somebody's band, getting yourself a record contract, going on tour, everybody did that. I was interested in chasing that too, at first. The West Coast seemed so much more thrilling though, so bright, so much sun to chase and bake in. So there I was and there I went with every dream fully promised to sprout. But I was no dummy. I mean, I did have an education, right? I graduated from the Music Conservatory in Boston. I had demos and résumés and every plan they taught me. Right? Stephen Lucas, my old buddy from Sturtevant Street with whom I had grown up, landed out there a few months before me, so I had begun a tight circle of contacts. I had some other distant cousins out there too. We would go out there and see them every other year or so when I was growing up. My cousin Devonne, my mom's sister's only child—who is a trip, I tell ya—she was there. Devonne would always keep in touch, claiming "The sun don't shine in December making your back warm for nothing—something good's going on out here, Cuz." So my inclination was to head where I might have some of that light. I just figured I'd move that far from the Midwest where I had grown up just to get a fresh start, a new perspective: the West was *way* different, especially for music.

CEDRIC'S TRUTH: THE KIDS ON STURTEVANT STREET

I never really moved with the whole jazz clique they indoctrinated you into at the East Coast schools. I really dreamed of being a songwriter, and in Los Angeles there seemed to be plenty of doors which at that time I had hoped would just swing open for me. I hit a brick wall fast, though. I never will forget those first weeks trying to get someone to hear my work. In New York everything was so secretive. You waited and waited, some sad secretary talking to you like you were a nobody. The East Coast deal brokers seemed so mysterious about the industry, as if they were always hiding something, a contract or industry contact. You might think California would be an even harder place to really break into, but at the time, I just melted in with the vibe, the way people were. It just seemed more laid back. Right after finishing school, I needed that. For some reason just seeing those palm trees paints in your psyche a kind of chill feel. The first break I got was from some contact I had through an old school chum who introduced me to this guy at BSire Records on Hollywood Boulevard. My friend told this record executive that I was a young songwriter-slash-producer who had a bunch of ready-made songs that could be used to frame some new singers. At this point, God, seemed every week there was some new sexy girl or guy singer to be made. No more bands, strangely, just singers, singers, and more singers. That's when it all changed. I mean, Jackson Five became Michael Jackson; Gladys Knight and The Pips became Gladys Knight; The Commodores became Lionel Ritchie; the Supremes became Diana Ross. It goes on and on. It's like someone just flipped a switch, or as the kids say, "flipped the script" and the music scene just seemed different overnight. Maybe at that point this was good.

I went to this exec's office and waited and waited, but the people seemed so friendly, all about not worrying, pleasant and chill. I thought, *I can live with this!* The receptionist, some blonde lady, cute, named Carry, was answering phones and taking folks in to see this exec guy, Josh Kinson, that I had the contact with. Seems this guy wanted to meet me, hear some music and give it a listen, right? The appointment was 4pm on a Monday. I was dressed in my linen pants, a white shirt, and loafers, briefcase in one hand and a big bright blue Panasonic tape player in the other. I was ready! Carry announced,

"Mr. Sullivan, Josh can see you now." She popped her gum, looked at her fingernails and proceeded to escort me to her boss down a long corridor. As I walked that long hall, everything became slow motion, more dramatic.

The entrance to the office seemed ten miles away. The carpet had a single long red stripe straight up the middle that made the already endless nervous walk seem like torture. On the walls on both sides hung all kinds of records under glass, framed NARAS awards for sales, and pictures of this guy I was to see. Photo after photo of this guy with stars, recording artists, some of whom I recognized. He hung out with everybody in the industry and was industry-grounded for sure. Why was I here? What was I doing? Well, I got myself ready. I had actually been waiting and planning for this for the last five years. The anticipation of being called after all this time of dreaming, to actually walk into someone's office and present my music makings—wow. The songs I had ready to go were fully produced with rhythm section, horns, myself on piano, and some great singers on vocals. I felt a surge of confidence. I walked in.

He was a young middle aged white guy, tanned of course, sun glasses on top of his head, peach shirt, white pants, gym shoes. While he was there to see me, he seemed distant, like a salesman rather than the sunny L.A. record producer or executive I had imagined. But he was there and I had come to share.

"Good afternoon, Cedric, it's a pleasure to meet you. We've heard a lot about your work from Morris. Welcome also to Los Angeles. Beautiful out here, huh?" I felt warmed.

"Why, thank you, Mr. Kinson."

"Don't call me mister, just Josh, man, please."

"Thank you for the gracious offer to let me play my music for you. I know you have lots of folks you must be seeing."

"You're right, I do, but right now I'm seeing *you*."

He cordially stepped from behind his desk to shake my hand and asked, "What do you have for us today, Cedric? I'm really looking for a sound for acts that will sell. Morris tells me you are quite a talented writer and producer. Did you play everything on this demo?"

CEDRIC'S TRUTH: THE KIDS ON STURTEVANT STREET

The idea that he was first and foremost interested in a sound to sell didn't shock me too much, but that "playing everything" got me. I mean, I produced a first-rate music demo with live horns, singers, full production. My models were Motown, Quincy, or Norman Connors, but the game had changed. We were in the eighties now, where one guy pushed all the buttons, programmed the machines, and projected a more singular, slick, produced, and polished version of new artistry. "We've got a couple new gals, and a boy band or two, really sweet looks. So I'm really looking beyond the L.A. crew for my next sounds. Gotta have something fresh for delivery, know what I mean?"

My stomach began to ache, but I fought through it. *Maybe it's just because this is my first bite,* I thought to myself. I didn't know I had already been bitten into.

He reached over for my tape demo, and as I let go of it I could just feel a piece of me dying, knowing I was handing over a precious idea of love to a salesperson who seemed to have an itchy, sweaty hand, anxious for a sound or style I was going to lend him, at a cost.

I don't know, maybe it was the way the office was set up. A window gave a view of billboards and advertising, sunny day but foggy sky. On his desk there were pictures of his kids, no wife anywhere, a diet Pepsi, and pistachio nuts. There was no music anywhere. Everything just seemed so pristine, ready-made, with the life pressed out of it. There was no spilled juice anywhere. A New York office? There was stuff on the desks, records and tapes on the floors, music blaring everywhere, and people going from desk to desk answering telephones. It was a crazed maze, but while it seemed closed, it still opened my mind to imaging those mysterious offices were busy with the business of discovering talent. This guy was here to sell a pretty product. It just never occurred to me, selling a product. I wasn't thinking about it like that.

He listened and I sat there and he was looking out the window, tapping his pencil. After the first few minutes he asked, "So, what else you got?"

"Well, I have several more. What didn't you like about what you've heard so far?" My second mistake. I was too anxious about what he was looking for. My first mistake was that I trusted him to know music. I urged him to fast forward to the next tune. In those days, there was no digital, no track numbers; people had to sit there and be interested, or so you hoped. Well, he didn't like anything. Nothing rubbed him as having a right fit for the projects he'd had in mind. I, surprisingly, was not discouraged. This was my first industry meeting, but I was sure this guy wasn't *hearing* what I was making for music, at least at that point. I would later figure this out: the business is not run by people who care or know anything about music. They were attorneys, business suits, and salespeople looking for the dollar value of their investment. The Ahmet Ertugens, Jerry Wexlers, Chess Brothers, Berry Gordys were gone. Needless to say, I left there thinking "Bye-bye, Mr. Record Executive," and this would be a song I'd sing time and time again. I wish I had a dollar for every talented songwriter who came to L.A. looking for a record deal, looking to be taken in, used and put out there by that industry. After months and months of sunshine-faced record executives, I slowly began to feel my insides changing; my soul was becoming soured by the juice of an industry that promised something on TV it wasn't planning on delivering to anyone. I began to see the recording industry wasn't making the music that we were brought up to believe in. This was the beginnings of a different need and reason for music, and it ached and troubled me from deep inside—it still does. I was clearly not having a purple "reign," but a rather Blue cloud. I mean, we were facing all kinds of things exploding mega–culturally, you know, you were there too. We all felt the tremors.

L.A. Love and Romance 1983

"It's like a jungle, sometimes it makes me wonder how I keep from going under."

That line held some truth for me. On the one hand there was the kind of "ghetto rage" that was brewing in the perhaps poetic sensibilities of a Grandmaster Flash, but as far as I was concerned, it was the creative real musicians' work of something like The Police, Synchronicity that let us know music still had the pulse of pointing. We had great diversity of music in those post-college years of the 1980's and that propelled me and my development.

To make music, I played in some top-forty wedding bands and worked as busboy at some swank downtown café. After two or three years of this, of being in the L.A. music industry abyss, I started doing substitute teaching in the public school system. I didn't plan it that way, but after months and months of no record deals, no studio gigs, no real way in as I had hoped, I thought, *You gotta eat*. At least I could respectably pay my bills, and the hours weren't bad. I could still make gigs at night when I got them, I could have some appointments during the day.

I remember those kids. Yuck. I hated teaching at first. I wasn't ready to focus on others, especially others' kids. But you know what? I began to discover a bit of myself in those kids who were seeing music as a way out. That rap crap had begun and everybody wanted to do their own thing, produce demos, and all this chase-the-industry stuff. I often think back to when Marvin Gaye was shot, I was so sure we were headed into Crazyville. I thought, *Who would keep the songs going on, going on, going on?* Desmond Tutu was awarded a Nobel Peace Prize and it was that news from these years that allowed glimpses of hope that others were out there doing the work that those years proceeding us had prepared us for. Music was still there to point, but those kids wanted to get around the music to get to what was going to make them famous or whatever.

I couldn't accept this idea, and I fought it. I could teach others to fight this too, inspire them as I had been inspired. That idea gave me new energy, and I seized it. I did begin to love teaching, and some real responses started to happen as we worked together, 'cause we did school shows and all. I mean it was nothing to call the boys back East about, but hey, I was doing something and my music was somewhat connected and central to all of it. I was in the Pasadena public schools teaching as a substitute music teacher by day and playing gigs by night, making demos of my songs and shooting into the L.A. scene where I could.

It was this time period and my meeting a love for the first time that changed my life forever.

I remember it well. Stephen invited me to a party. I had been living in Pasadena for about a year, hanging, trying to plug in where I could. On the evening of the party, I drove up to this house on California Boulevard, and as the music seeped from the house, my mind began to associate those sounds of the music immediately with a call to deal with the emptiness that was brewing inside of me; there was no love in there. Months of moving, working, chasing the broken dream, teaching, had me shaken up; I had no real consistent social life whatsoever. Maybe I was a freak or something. Never mind the fact that nobody at the time was talking about anything but what *they* were about, trying to be this success story or that one, or getting with this one to get over on that one. I just wasn't into all that snob hob, card-passing stuff. I wasn't interested in what job I could get, or who I needed to see or get with.

I walked into that party and there was an amazing vibe happening, music slamming—Earth Wind and Fire, "Let's Groove," of course.

"Hey, bro," Stephen greeted me as soon as I got there. Folks were over in the corner, talking; I was scoping the rooms, up the stairs, seeing couples, poking my head into dark rooms, smelling cigarette and weed smoke. I hate cigarettes, but I smelled that somebody had made some Mexican food downstairs, which I adored. I was trying to seem inconspicuous, grooving, walking and moving towards whatever food I could find. "Man, Cedric. Did you see all that fine foxiness coming and going? Riding high and smooth from the back jack! Whooo-wee!"

"No, I missed that one, bro."

Using his hands to trace an imaginary and highly *curvaceous* figure, he said, "Let's just say she clearly had all of Africa's blessings in all sets of her *genes*. Can you dig it, bro?"

"Be right back, Steve. Let me grab some grub, bro."

All I saw and surveyed was the layout. It was a great night, really. I needed that, and I needed to hang with some Black people, grooving. There is nothing like our folks in a groove together. I finally squeezed through a group of folks dancing, getting past them to the kitchen where the food was being served. There was the table, piled high with delicious Mexican food, and of course, more folks were there, eating and talking.

Before I put anything on my plate, I had to reorder the arrangement of the foods, you know, so I could pile up the plate my way. It's got to taste and flow in order, right? I am not tripping, but just like in a movie, there was this lady, fine, down at the traditional punch bowl, seemingly alone. I felt like a deer with lights in eyes, and as I approached, I said to her, "Would hate you to loose your step here, let me get that for you so you don't drop your food." The words just came right out of my mouth. She could have been with any Bob and Doug there, I mean, she was a Tender-roni Brown, as they used to say. This sister was just an eyeful and particularly different from your regular party animal type. Turned out she was a recent transplant from the East, too. Our invites had come from a group of mutual friends who never intended to connect the two of us. Just then Stephen ran over, interrupted and made his best case for the "Oh, I never thought about this, you are both new in town spiel" to save face.

"Michelle Broaden, this is my dear friend, Cedric Sullivan, a great musician and writer. We grew up together."

He gave me the "Yo, bro, this one is single, you all should get to know one another" look. Didn't matter, I was already on it. For some reason, she knocked me off pitch at sight. I was hearing tunes from all kinds of places and it was just the way she graciously placed her cup down, took a bite of food, wiped the corner of her mouth with the napkin, placed the plate down, wiped her hands with another napkin, noticed another song just starting from the DJ's corner, pulled her hair back behind her ears, never taking an eye off me. In the most coordinated sweep she said, "Hi. It occurred to me that you were an artist, just the way you had waited and lined all your selections up like you were working a theme or something. You go on now, brother!"

I was stunned. This sister had peeped me before I even made it to the punch bowl and stumbled upon her. Forget the fact that she was astute enough to notice "theme and order." But check me out, I had no clue she was a dancer either when I said, "I would hate you to lose your step here." Well, she noticed that too.

"Isn't it funny you should make mention of me being in step, or not? Steve was about to tell you, I am a dancer."

Like Daisy in Fitzgerald's novel, "she had the kind of voice that the ear follows up and down as if speech was an arrangement of tones that will never be played again." She had the scent of a sweet ocean breeze that lingers as you are sprayed softly, but it stays deeply with you, it penetrates your senses, you live in it. Something was choreographed here. God, I am sure of it. I *love* dancers, you know. Friend, this was the beginning of one of my last dances with romance.

Michelle worked as a waitress, but also participated in a community dance-theater funded by a community college in her neighborhood. She had a small flow of young dancers she coached who were from the local middle and high schools. Her apartment in the neighboring of town Altadena had a nicely kept community activities room, and the landlord allowed her to use the room on weekends to work with these young ladies. Word of mouth and a fairly engaged arts community provided her with a steady flow of private students.

This meeting of Michelle shaped me newly, locked me into a new environment, and it was this experience that my destiny was inextricably bound with. A woman, a partner can give you that sense that your human self is fitting into life. Love gives lift to living. Not long after that choreographed dance with Michelle, we began to see each other regularly. Not long after that, I was sure we were falling in Love. I'd finish teaching and we'd meet for late afternoon lunch, fun things like a movie, or a walk in a park, attending an outdoor concert with a picnic basket. I just decided to be a human for once, and music got shut down; all the pursuits of the fame and discovery chase were silenced for now.

She was my first love. It was going to be the kind of love that stains a boy's fragile, crisp, white collar and that later chokes him, leaving him with no breath and a stake in his heart, and when he remembers those days he dies again a thousand sad deaths. Yeah, it was that kind of love.

My first fair lady actually had a Masters in dance from New York University, but soon after her graduation ended up following some old boyfriend out West; he in turn was found to have impregnated a younger woman. Well, that was that. Michelle turned inward, concentrated on finding solace among a network of women who worked to empower females and organized weekly sessions, movies, dinners. We attended many of these, and it was through those gatherings that she was approached by the director of the arts theater and dance troupe that was given a regular rehearsal space in the college's auditorium and concert hall. Somewhere in this mix, she got the idea that a private school could be funded, and maybe some of the patrons of the theater and company would think the connection beneficial. Maybe this could be a young artists' training camp? Of course I was drafted to help. Life got filled up with these worthy pursuits and I was provided with another human place to fit into. You learn in the arts you have to operate from many bases of strategic alliances to forge sustainability. We had a lot in common in this way. I wasn't so interested at first in a school, but working with all these youth ignited a slow flame that was to eventually create many fires which would never be put out, not to this day. Los Angeles was not exactly a place kind to such august ideas, and we talked often about environments that were more suited to non-commercial artist training.

"Ced," as she called me, "we could bring such focus to so many young lives here." Focus on young lives was at this point something I considered a nice respectable backdrop to the main stage of my pursuit of my music. This idea of creating a school began to sink in and I became seduced, taken over by her sincere desire to work with young people. We made a plan together. It had been months of a relationship, bonding, now a partnership, an engagement of our lives to securing funding for this youth arts camp-school-company thing. We named it Y.A.D.I. for Young Artists' Development Incorporated. The idea was to secure funding, move into a building, and recruit students from the local schools, give them training; many could even intern on weekends with Michelle's theater group. I would work on their music skills; we'd teach them how to design sets, write their scripts, choreograph—the whole nine yards. At first the numbers didn't match the efforts, but the purpose did, and a purpose held up long outlives any numbers. Soon, though, the numbers came too, and we grew.

In the afternoons and on Saturdays, my recruits from the public schools and her dancers would meet, and it was on. Within weeks, we had created an environment for these young artists and imbued them with a real sense of purpose for their work. The community theater gave us all a space and a show or two, matinees in their season. We were making beautiful music and life together. I was finding my soul.

But it hit. There were tax cuts in education, community arts funding was removed, the theater lost its support from the community college, and we were midway through the 80's Reagan Ranch. Soon thereafter, in 1987, the Dow Jones drop hit us all. Kind of all sickly cemented, the way it represented that our whole system spins on a capital gains for the corporate mains, and that if it shakes from the top, you ain't staying nor maintaining. Sadly, the public schools' arts and music programs were cut. I lost my job. Michelle's kids' parents pulled them from the after school lessons; people were losing jobs, families had no money for frills like music and art.

CEDRIC'S TRUTH: THE KIDS ON STURTEVANT STREET

This was stressful because there was nothing we could do. Within a year or so, Michelle became totally disillusioned, distant it seemed. I was beginning to drift as well, spending much of my time writing, moving deeper actually, sometimes creating all kinds of characters in my mind. I started believing in them, and those characters became my faith soldiers, preparing us for a battle.

One day, I was coming home from school—I was now a floating sub, which is just short for baby sitting for absent or sick teachers—and I stopped off at a local restaurant to pick up some food. I saw Michelle sitting in this diner, laughing it up across from this slick suit. I was thinking, "What is this craziness?" I went over to them. Just as gracious as always, without drama, Michelle introduced me to Reginald Lowry. Turned out he was some business attorney whom she contacted for advice on constructing a plan for investors in the school, our business. "Oh, I see, I get it." I did not like this guy.

Lowry Slick Suit slid in and out of cool daddy gestures to business savvy, and always made references to his work in this state or that one as if someone was supposed to know about it or him. "My Virginia case this" or "my Chicago client that." He represented all that we were at that time as a culture beginning to slide towards valuing: a slick sales pitch. He was the kind of guy who put it all together, a guy who could wear plaid, stripes, and circles all at once and didn't have to explain. His order was right, but he was crooked from the inside. He made my stomach ache on sight, but I buried my resentment and my better sense and went along, since Michelle was sure he was going to see us through this necessary business navigation. Somehow, business without a sincere soul strikes me as a recipe for disaster. Suddenly, Reginald was always around; we met regularly, working on an approach to go to local investors and foundations. Why not? Big business was by this time becoming a king in global markets, writing the life prescriptions for culture now. Why not get these assholes to do something correctly, right? I went along with all this with suspicion; remember, I never liked this slick suit. Michelle, though, oh my goodness, she never saw him as phony. She was all into this idea and had to meet with Reginald every other day, it seemed. Many times I arrived after they had already been planning together. I never saw it coming, although I could smell a soured soup stewing way back in the back of the back kitchen.

I remember one of those meetings which still brings heat between my temples when I think about it. "Ced," she always said during those times with a poetic ring of "look out for what's coming behind this."

"Ced, Reginald and I were thinking that maybe the school could get better funding in another county or state."

"Oh, really? What state had you all been thinking about?" He always had all the answers completely thought out.

"Well, Ced, my brother, hope you don't mind if I borrow the lady's affectionate short for you?" he said. Always a sure bet there was a knife under the blanket with this guy. He continued. "We think that, well, after reviewing the proposal, that there might be some better funding opportunities in states that have a more secure history of arts extra-curricular support. This may be a real pay-off."

"Yeah, but had you all considered the relationships we've already established here that may fruit just because we stayed around and were seen as contributing to this community? That may be a pay-off, too," I retorted.

Michelle was so accommodating to us both, as if we had equal interests here.

"You're' right, Ced, but Reginald has contacts for us that already have fruited in the way of funding opportunities for new arts-based community efforts. The West is wide, Ced! Maybe there are other cities, communities that, well, you know, the school may work better in."

He, Slick Suit Reginald started up again. "I certainly can do some more digging, send for one of you to come down and meet the folks, and this might give us a clearer picture of what the real deal is. Know what I'm saying, Cedric?"

A clearer picture of what the real deal was? This kind of second agenda rationale became the norm and I had fewer and fewer things to say that either of them wanted to hear. I never saw it coming. My music made me deaf to the new beats that were blaring loudly all around me.

CEDRIC'S TRUTH: THE KIDS ON STURTEVANT STREET

Michelle would come over some days and be jotting down ideas, and running over facts and figures, and I, well, I never seemed to factor in this new planning bliss. "What do you think about this?" "But Reginald says that." Then there were the annoying calls at all times of the day and night from Mr. Slick Suit, especially when we were together. I had had it. I wasn't going for it anymore, this thing was overtaking us. I was still working in the schools, she was waiting on tables, and the rest of the free time was spent working on this proposal. The business plan was budgeted out to cover administrative assistants, teachers, space rental, equipment, and salary lines for an executive assistant and two directors. There was as well a budget line for legal advisory, yep, Reginald. I could understand a fee for one-time consultation, which was standard. But this line was ongoing, like he was going to be around regularly. I was not having it! When I approached Michelle about it, it was just graciously danced around ever so delicately.

"Oh, Ced," she'd say, "you are just listening to the wrong characters in your mind. They are singing you the wrong songs. I love you, come on. I just have got to get this right for us."

That sounded as correct as a cold mouse in warm soup. I was asking about financial matters; what did Love have to do with this?

Oh.

But it was too late. She was long gone. Someone had taken my ballerina and choreographed her right from under my nose while I was learning the wrong dances. I couldn't hear the changes.

Some say it's really healing to realize you are not anywhere near perfect figuring this relationship thing out, and that in those moments you really move toward being more human with yourself. Well, hell, it hurt, and yes, I felt stupid. If that's what being human was about, I should have moved to Mars! For years, my poetic mind blocked my pain by painting her as the type of woman who would cut you and lick the blood off the blade. I really couldn't understand why people behaved the way they did, but when I factored in the idea of human brokenness, people working through their stuff, it got me closer to working through the why. I surmised that, due to no fault of her own, there was some brokenness within her.

In the worldwide context, Tiananmen Square students were getting rolled over, and the Berlin Wall was falling, so what did it all mean? My world was changing and so was the rest of the world. It was the end of the eighties. While others were dancing through it, I fell out of connection with my music, in love, then out of love, and I was about to be tripped into the 90's with no clue as to where I would end up! Culturally, I felt I was in isolation from a deeper picture of myself. In Los Angeles, people were all around, floating their faces, lifestyles. Why do you think they created this place and then called it Hollywood? So everybody could act, pretend, and be seen as holy. Anyway, it was over. I hated Hollywood. So there it was. I had focused two years on building this plan, this partnership, leaving many of my own goals on a back burner that didn't even work, and I now had to find my center again.

Claude's: The Last Dance

"Ced, you can't change the direction the rain falls or how life was written."

So Michelle, besides being a hussy and a gold-digger, became a philosopher, too. Now I had a new focus. I had to figure out who "me" was. I had to *rediscover* me. I started writing again, busying myself making demos, performing, and trying to reignite my connections.

I began to think a lot about songs, what they say, and what they do for us. I noticed that love as a quality and condition of life is rarely sought in the song lyric. It hit me then, and I started to revamp some old songs of mine, using my pain as an existential creative plus. It worked. Songs serve to connect people to inner, not external, sources: soul, sentiment, sense, and sound. I believed my songs were grounded in the stuff that matters, and I thought more about having singing products out there that connected and deeply inspired.

There was no need to move my not-so-fair lady out, or me move—the fact that we were not living together made this part of the tragic cadence resolve quite naturally. I didn't have to see her face or move away. It was devastating to say the least, but all young men fall in love and get hurt. It is part of the becoming a man. I moved on to focus on my music and develop other interests. I survived her.

It was about this time in the mid to late eighties that I began to be attracted to Leirmert Park, at Degnan and 43rd, near Crenshaw Boulevard, on the city's West side. It was a real draw for the musicians, artists, poets, and creative adventurous types, counter-cultural even, with clubs, coffee shops, and poetry hangs, real artsy. Degnan

Street was Black, too, and the street proudly boasted determination, ownership, community, and creativity down to the concrete, baby! I was on home soil here, at Sika's and the World Stage Gallery, and at the park where you could stroll and talk "bad-ass get-down." You can still go there today and musicians and such still hanging out, simply being. It has that *feel*, like those kinds of places where artists deal with one another and do their *thing*. I began hanging out there with a group of dedicated musicians who really believed in taking care of one another. My good friend Stephen was among this crowd. They met in the storefront of one of the musicians' family. This group of musicians felt that not only did their work demand an audience and club support, but that there needed to be extended support established, fan lists, food care, and health care for working musicians.

I found this quite curious. They pooled some of their money and set up accounts to which they contributed to from a series of gigs, business and foundation dances that were beginning to be big.

Businesses, while snubbing arts and education, certainly liked to party it up, and who was going to play all that shake-butt music? The bands! While DJing had begun to put musicians out of work, the die-hard partying community from the seventies crowd still valued live bands. This may have been the "last party" for us, but we were on-call for every weekend hit. While the music was backdrop for these stiff businessman corporate types, I was immersed again in making music for people, and doing it in community with real musicians. I loved that, and I was reintroduced to my paths.

We began playing regularly at a place called Claude's. We would pack them in there. The elitist, tall ticket prices for the "in" crowd, Studio 54 drug culture thing that the discotheques of the mid seventies created in New York, L.A., and other big cities wasn't for us. The deal here was that musicians could create their own environments where the music could spray forth, the vibe and the spirit would be there, and the people would come! That's the great gift music gives: it shares, it provides, it excites, it imagines and envisions, and it moves people. Claude's was packed every night, so we didn't need corporate sponsorship for what we believed in: the music.

CEDRIC'S TRUTH: THE KIDS ON STURTEVANT STREET

These guys and ladies decided to throw a benefit for a musicians healthcare fund. I found this hilarious, but it instilled in me a very important lesson. Stephen, George, Leonard, Ken, and Cat proposed a benefit concert in Claude's where they would invite many of the foundation business suits and entice them to contribute. Why not? The business and foundations community had been generous with their hiring and tips, and one could sense that the musicians were making in-roads with other potential outlets, like commercial jingles and ads, and even playing private parties at homes. We created a real musicians' service. All the guys swore these business suits and foundation ladies were all coming out and bringing their friends to support the effort. It was one of those off-shoot deals where, while their company or foundation mandates could not extend to such events, they themselves could bring well-connected well-wishers and folks who could write checks. This was to be a healthcare benefit for musicians—let's not forget that most musicians don't think about health, healthy environments, healthy eating, healthy working hours, or healthy living in general, thus the reasons for my chuckles at the very idea. This smoke-filled, late-night bar was to host an event for the greater cause of healthcare? Right.

Claude's was a classic bar-dive in a beginning-to-be-broken neighborhood, but people still supported it. It was a staple place in the neighborhood, like a CBGB's in New York, the home of punk in the mid seventies. It was dark inside, despite the 70's lights, you know, those disco bar lights they'd hang up. A strobe light alternatively pointed at the stage, the juke box, and a long line of drinking patrons whose stories were many and whose time was up. So many characters! There was a stage, a pretty good sound system, and people who liked music, of course.

Patrick, the owner, was a kind of crusty fellow who you could swear was in the mob or something. He would act as the emcee, announcing the acts from the stage. Patrick was a business man. He once told me, "Ced, I don't give a bat's brown balls about all that artful playing. As a mater of fact, I wish you all didn't play so well, 'cause if it's too good, the people stay around and listen too much. I want them to eat, drink and leave so more tables can be turned over."

Well, that was Patrick, but I liked him because he taught me about the basics of business. "You have to have something that draws people, you have to give them something and convince them, like when you're selling food, that it tastes good and that they *need* it, and they need to come back here another time." That's how Patrick schooled me about the practical side of the business. He was direct. It was not about music at all. "Beyond all the art-shit stuff, people are basic, friend. They want to hear something that just moves them, like a fix, and that's OK. Got it, Ced?"

I had to start in on my sell first, though, and Patrick was a real piece of work! Before giving in to my "music for the minds" idea he would begin:

"What are you going to do to promote music happening on these nights?

"What kind of sales at the door are you going to promise for these nights?

"The proper right music question is: how many people are you going to get to show up?"

I would glare and pound back, "Our work here should *never* be about the sales at your door. I see the importance of music at Claude's is how it makes money for you. I don't like it, nor agree, but I understand. The first problem with your line of thinking is that it is not our job to promote anything. The musicians are hired to play music. That's it." Patrick never heard anything about music, but rather what it did to keep his bottom line. "I don't hear the value of music in my cash register right now. The only thing I value, Youngblood, is the rhythm of the swing of that cash register when my customers buy, buy, buy. What can you do to make sales, Captain Cedric?"

I couldn't help myself. "My rationale as an artist is that what I bring to you, the music, has value, the performance provides you and your customers with all the value you need. That's what you are paying your musicians for, the value they bring with their artistry. You have to be willing to accept and appreciate that as value, in the same way you see the value in paying for expensive artwork, or having the best wine or olive oil there for your customers."

"Olive oil?! What kind of weed you been smoking, kiddo? The only oil I use is Crisco for the fries, honey." He was classic, that Patrick of Claude's. "I need a guarantee man, how many asses in my seats keep my lights on?"

I wasn't mad at him, just disappointed in this way of thinking. I couldn't ever survive with those types of chains on me. My music and professional association were worth too much to succumb to that kind of thinking, but I understood quickly that that's what business began to call for. Must have been something he saw in me beneath all that being a heavy, youthful obstinate. I think he saw some of himself, his ambition in my self-created formula, because I got the gig for our gang and was happy to succumb to his regular rants just as he put up with me.

"Ced, my man." Patrick would say, with the cigarette blasting smoke in my face, the cigarette which hung so low, clinging to his lips, you'd think it's—it's—it's going to drop out any minute, but it never did. He must have had glue on that butt. "Ced, that table over there hasn't turned over yet, 'cause the musicians' solos are too long. Short solos, Ced, short sets. Wrap it up, wrap it up, get 'em out of here. Now *that's* how you get them to come back hungry for more the next time, and they'll bring a few more friends.

"Music means nothing to me, Ced. I don't even *like* music, but it's good for business. It's only another activity that keeps people interested in coming here and buying—food, alcohol, and music. Thanks for the music, Ced. I have kids who want to go to college, Ced, and you're helping 'em. Hey, why don't I give you my kid's books when he graduates, how about that? In the midst of all this economic and political turmoil, where were the artists, poets for me, Ced?" He could never really understand my passion for music, or just the whole reason of things, but I loved him anyway. When I think back on my old buddy Patrick, I feel a warm spot in my chest. He was down to the rare earth about it.

The whole benefit plan seemed like a decent formula. Doing a benefit for the musicians who were a part of community, keeping it at home at Claude's was a good thing. Patrick walked away, but I know he always liked me. I didn't mind. I knew that despite his brusqueness, Patrick understood to some degree. As long as the band was tight, and people were loving it, it was all good.

One night, hanging in Claude's during a gig, I noticed a fascinating woman dancing a fancy Cuban two-step quite on-beat with a young man almost a third her age. She had a *look*, and the way she moved intrigued me. All my friends noticed my interest and stare.

"Hey, man!" One of the guys pulled me off to the side. "Do you know Samantha Hunn?"

"No," I said.

"Ced, my brother, let me tell you. *She's* a story."

She wore a tight, well-made, sequined violet dress, which shimmered and glittered, hanging to just above her knees. I never made eye contact with her. She danced in swirls. As the younger man circled closer, he laughed nervously, but delighted, like he was dancing with his mother—or maybe she was a cougar out on the hunt? Stephen, never missing a beat, noticed me checking this out. "That's a rich lady, bro. She got a move, huh? She's here all the time."

Though Claude's was dimly lit, I imagined what she looked like up close. I still hadn't met this woman, even though we were there every weekend. I got distracted for a moment, lost her for a time, and by the time I noticed her again, she was dancing with another woman, equally thrilled and bewitched by this cougar lady with her suave dance moves. Another conversation with friends ensued.

"Cedric, have you met Ambassador Hunn yet?"

"No, damn it, I keep telling you guys. Who is this woman?" I asked.

"She's a trip, man. Real rich lady, was married to the director of the dance company here in Leimert Park."

"Really?" I said, now more intrigued.

"Yeah, she's loaded, bro, like a stuffed sweet potato. She may look old and wrapped in rough skin, but she's *way* hot, on fire." I watched her with greater captivation. I wondered if she would give us money or just dance to our beats. In those days, Claude's had these kinds of characters. Claude's was an odd mix of personalities, music, bohemia, revolutionaries, and flashes of fancy people to ponder. I loved Claude's because my music could live there.

"You keep doing it, brother!" an older bar regular shouted at me as I passed by. "Y'all keeping the notes right and the beats tight...I like that, yeah!" Then in a dash, Ambassador Hunn whisked by me, alone. I decided in a second of craziness and curiosity to finally say something, so I stopped her swirling.

"Excuse me, Ambassador Hunn, your dancing is so exquisite, when I'm playing up there, just watching you makes me stay on the beat." They always love the musicians.

She stopped swirling for a moment. "Why, aren't you about as cute as they come, Mr. Musician. I recognize you from up there now, since I'm seeing this close." She used two of her long fingers to illustrate, pointing from her eyeballs to mine. I was bent into another key. I never saw age in her face or felt ill in her demeanor. She had the kind of classic beauty, like how you see in those old movies. Her eyes seemed to hold infinite intelligence and cunning. I knew why the boys got trapped.

"I'll be listening more closely now, but, hun, I gotta run, friends calling. Sing a song just for me, I'll be listening." She pulled at her ear and winked. Then she swirled away. I had to start telling myself that every note I played was for the musicians' healthcare fund and not for her, definitely not for her. I had to keep saying this with my characters.

Artists create community, not commerce. I was starting to believe that we were that fighter figure that championed what people held and valued and fought for in their hearts. For those business suits attending that night, though, the bottom line was their friend until the end. They were always trying to undermine our work by saying it was merely *entertainment*. For them, all of us came from a fancy bottle with a logo, which they could stock when they were ready for it. Patrick I could tolerate, but those corporates really, truly bothered me.

Those business people rubbed me the wrong way, but they did nothing to dampen the liveliness of the party. The food there, the chicken wings and fries, burgers, coleslaw, hot sauce. The smell of cigarettes, which I still hated, hot fried grease and alcohol created an impression of an unhealthy but fun place. Anyway, we played several sets. We jammed and funked down. I was making music again and connecting with my downbeats. The critical lesson I learned was about what music making could mean in community. You have to have a band; that's how you create ritual and joy and meaning in music; it's when artists do their thing together that it really connects in all ways, no matter what the "thing" is. That was good, that was very good. We played the benefit concert at Claude's for ourselves, but the business suits and those valued locals who came out got to hear too.

I played piano and sang; there were guitarists, bass players, percussionists, four horn players, and three singers. No DJ, no rapper, no dancers, no big screens—just the music. The pop of that snare drum, the wind lines from those horns were like the harmonious breath of a community. The backbeat and scratch of that rhythm section—unbelievable. That's the best stuff. That's the tradition where soul and funk were the order of the day. That concert brought the kind of moment artists talk about as euphoric. There is that moment in performance where it all comes together. All those music lessons, practice sessions, all those rehearsals, all that music you listened to and all those conversations you had with friends about music, all those things matter because a stream of sound, ideas, and experiences was created and it moved people. It's kind of spiritual in the sense that you're in another place, and that expression, that spray of sound and light that drives the experience, is what everyone connects to. It's beyond everybody. We are all caught in the inescapable thrill, and *that's it*, the musicians are channeling something and they know it. When that's blocked, then the people can't get to the drinking well, you force them to go dry at the throat, then they become coarse, cutthroat even. So we don't want the music to stop. And that night, what mattered to me beyond the material benefits was the music-making. That's what we made that night at Claude's: ritual. We were all in the holy note moment. Ambassador Hunn swirled and levitated all night. That's when music matters, baby!

The day after the benefit, the local paper read:

> "Last night, Claude's local pub, eatery and sometimes music house was home to a gang of musicians

who have been lifting the rafters off for weeks on end. This motley crew perfected an already-seasoned stomp with a funky mix of top forties, jazz, and superb arrangements, which brought the house to a frenzy. A secondary cause, hardly felt, was a call to provide monies as a benefit for a worthy, albeit idealistic attempt to create a musicians' fund for health care. Hardly a healthy environment, but a healthy cause for sure. Nevertheless, the music survived the cause and Claude's remained, if not only in the heart and ears, in the feet and rears of those attending who wailed, danced, and beat their hands on bar stools to the drive of this menacing musical unit. Bravo to Claude's and their pulsating programming, says this reviewer."

We raised about four hundred dollars, just enough for us to buy salads, purified water, some tofu, yogurt, and a subscription to musicians' magazine. But a useable, sustainable healthcare fund? I don't think so. There was a 200 dollar check signed by S. Hunn, but none of the expected corporate business suits showed in numbers or contributed greatly. None of them seemed to care about the better well-being of our causes, except of course as entertainment.

"Ced, Ced, you drew a crowd, baby!" Patrick seemed happy. "I'm pleased as peaches growing in Paradise!" He sold a lot of fried chicken and drinks that night.

"Thanks Patrick. You rolling, baby. The band was loving it." I told him that, but I felt differently. I sold my art to another bidder, and while Patrick provided the space, my characters within me were once again restless. Puffing on that cigarette that choked me, Patrick shared, "Ced, you're not like them. I watched a generation and a half of them come and go." I wasn't quite sure who he was talking about, so I leaned in and listened again. "You know the types, Ced, don't you? Those business bean counters." I couldn't believe it. Was the pot calling the kettle black? He ranted on. "You see, Cedric, I'm different, I'm like you. You and me, we sing our own songs," he laughed, "because them, they believe that corporation downtown there envisioned, dreamed, created their go-getter spirit and provided all their opportunities and advances. Me? No, never did do that. Like I say, I'm like you."

I sat silent.

"You see, Ced, they didn't believe enough in what we believe, that the worth of your *do*, what you get done out here, is based on your ability to create and manage your own world. See them bar stools over there? They match with them pictures over there. Same color as the plates we use. That's what I saw in a dream one night. You get it?"

Well, I never felt any of the charms assembled as decorative taste in Claude's were moving. But I got his point, they were *his*. "You see, Ced, like I been saying to you, son. The ability to make your own way is the greatest gift of all. That's what we do at Claude's. That don't come from no corporate company downtown, Ced. Make your own good first, let them add to you. Don't chase to be placed, that's death, Ced."

For the first time I really understood how I connected to Patrick. Although he dreamed strange colors in another dream land, he still had dreams.

I got the sense that the educational cuts we witnessed in that era were just like the business suits who seemed happy as they danced and financed their dream projects: those people couldn't care less about the meaning of our lives and work. It seemed to me that the industry turned its eyes away from what the music meant to people and resorted to turning music solely into cash flow. Following the cuts on education and culture, big business began to look to music as a dance, a dance that whirled them into entertaining bliss. They named it disco, and some claimed it was short for the death of music. It was OK music, well-produced, well-performed, but the function was just to sell a fleeting moment of dance. And worst of all, it was decided upon by the corporates. Artists hate that! I suddenly found myself serving a function that had been reconstructed for and by corporate interests, and was bombarded with opportunities to sell my good sound to the corporate dance hall. I wasn't having it, and yet many musicians had to fall in line with that in order to work, to *be* musicians.

CEDRIC'S TRUTH: THE KIDS ON STURTEVANT STREET

When the economy soured, while we packed Claude's, Patrick, a gangster for sure, either got in some hot water or burned the club himself. He was pushed to abandon his dream. Soon thereafter, Claude's was gone. Funny, those musicians with all that unionized identity stuff were, in the end, still drawn in and pinned up with the phony worlds of promises of goodies from their corporate friends. They traded in their instruments for punch cards and computers. Some got married off to them, and our community was infiltrated with ideas which had little to do with being creative. I ran away from that crowd, fearing my very being and soul would be strangled and hung out to dry. I'd disintegrate, turn to dust, and be blown away by the whirl of mindless dancers lost in the beats driven by machines. Kool and the Gangs' "Celebration" seemed mindless. I hated it, and I was alone and lost in Hollywood in the eighties, my lost decade, in the place where the world looked to construct fantasies. I became more depressed. I couldn't teach, I had less and less gigs. I had hit rock bottom again and I had no plans for surfacing. I was wise enough during the fluid times to put away some money, from which I didn't draw, but after some time without regular pay, I had ignored my bill responsibilities, which mounted, and I was evicted from my apartment. I was too embarrassed to tell my cousin Devonne. I felt I couldn't face her. Stephen had gotten married and had three kids, so I couldn't go down that route. I eventually figured I could handle it by myself.

Sleeping in a shelter or outside for a few weeks in sunny California couldn't be all that bad. It was. I experienced firsthand a kind of poverty in the real living world, and it was no pretty poetry, but a picture of powerlessness. The lack of power you can't change. I couldn't take up that charge, really, it wasn't mine, but I was awake to see the nightmare. I was moved to never forget it, even though I couldn't really help. I could get out. I became, for a moment, for a chapter, the poor who live among us everyday, and my characters refused to be counted in. We *had* to do something. I dealt with my situation until I was able to grab a hold of the voices in my head, until I figured out what to do next.

Finding New Grounds

Life is a musical with songs that never stop modulating.

After those Los Angeles debacles left me with no fame, no fortune, no love, no house, no pillow to rest my head on, I began to ache from deep within.

I thought a lot about it, what I wanted to do, and I decided that my story was an important one. "No!" my characters said to me, "The story hasn't yet been written. Well, history, but what about *our* story?" What I had felt was that my characters were telling me that we all have to write a new story because the page we are all reading from is the wrong page. You still with me, friend? The new page needed to be written, and I would score the narrative. There was a community college that offered advanced Masters degree courses given in connection with an experimental urban program with state universities who participated. The Los Angeles community colleges are well known for being accessible and numerous. I still had some money saved, and I convinced them I could pay course by course and seek Masters studies in American History, specializing in social movements and music. I moved into a small shared-living apartment near the Hermosa-Redondo beach area with a group of young beachers. I took a job as a busboy. It was a great bohemian scene. I could lose myself and spend hours at the ocean, seeing life from other angles. My mind opened.

I too took great pride in my work, but believed deeply in my dreams, just like Langston Hughes did, working as a young poet and busboy at the Wardman Park hotel.

CEDRIC'S TRUTH: THE KIDS ON STURTEVANT STREET

You ever watch a sunset? I mean *really* watched it? Just sitting there, maybe on a beach, alone, watching the sun melt away into the horizon. It's like the horizon is a natural big-screen theater. I watched it one day thinking about this, and it seemed I could feel everything I thought I believed in like a setting sun, melting away into this new twist of things. These last decades seemed to change right before my eyes like that sunset. During that time, I began to wake up and smell the cappuccino. Living consciously in this time, you remember, right? Living through the sixties, seventies, then moving into the 80's, and now the 1990's was like watching all major values shift into gear, the time went out of tune, just changed tempo or the key. I would clip all the newspapers when big events hit, study them, and ask myself and my characters what was really happening. I kept all those old clippings in an old trunk. When I look back to those years, a lot went on. I just sat, and people watched. I got my lessons.

When I think about it, all the people I knew left their values back there, most of them ended up chasing the dreams to get goodies to make it into Made-it Land. That was it, and the new industries were their Promised Land, what with their business, technology, and such. All the while, Mr. Man was changing the plans again, and everybody was spinning and spending, thinking we were all winning. Each day after I entered the program, I busied myself in my studies, never looking up, just reading, reading, building my case as my characters, now fully informing me, led us to understand what was really going on in the world. Who would teach us, how would I begin to share this vision with others? It was at that point where I began to not despise Michelle for her transgressions, but I begin to appreciate what she had actually given me. The insight on education, the ennobling and enabling of young minds to be the bearers and sharers of the great news. The eighties pushed me and that was all.

Now the 90's were upon us. I call it the Spike Lee decade. *Do The Right Thing* opened up the decade, addressing the age-old questions of racial disharmony in America that were still in the mix. Man, I was so moved by his entrance into the scene. He could tell his narrative, and people were listening. He could be that funny little weird dude in his movie, *She's Gotta have It*, our Black Woody Allen who asked and dealt with the provocative, searing questions we had to drag ourselves through. *I could do that, someday, someway*, I thought, *but my way.*

I buried myself in asking some harder questions about living outside of my own directed dream. Through my studies I found the work of Woody Guthrie, Bob Dylan, Marley, Joan Baez, and Richard Wagner. I absorbed ideas about philosophy, culture, and society. During this time I found writers whom I cherished and who sought inspiration in the artistic strategies of musicians. Ralph Ellison, a musician himself, Toni Morrison, Cornel West even, found musicians' work, narratives, illuminating, even strategically imperative to their arguments, their hope to provide insights into the joy and tragedy of human experience followed by expression. And I then found strategies in the writers. I begin to phrase, sense, lift and play with meaning and form with the subtleties and longer views of writers and cultural critics. I found great solace and a oneness with the creative boundaries of their quiet, then busy, then explosive minds. I loved Richard Wright's poignant close of his early autobiography, *Black Boy*, which became one of my models. I know it by heart: "If this country can't find its way to a human path…conduct a deeper sense of life…all of us are going down the same drain. Humbly now with no vaulting dream of achieving a vast unity, I wanted to try to build a bridge of words between me and the world outside.. hurl words into darkness and wait for an echo, and if an echo sounded..I would send other words to tell, to march, to fight, to create a sense of the hunger for life that gnaws in us all, to keep alive in our hearts a sense of the inescapable human." Man, that was so powerful and beautifully put. What if our work were ideas that we tossed into the air, and expected them to be received because people recognized their real hunger for life and wanted to keep alive those impulses of the inescapable human? After I finished my studies, there was nowhere for me to go but away to test this. The culture in L.A. was entrenched in the high life and was not suited to facilitate what I began to see as a real need to train young people in using their gifts to change the world. I needed to head back to the Midwest, to a place that would support this work. Hell, I didn't know what work I would do, but I knew I had to get out there. Out there, back in the Midwest, they might hear.

Indiana 1993-2001: Allen Academy

"The Allen Arts Academy in Indianapolis is looking for a full-time music history teacher. We are looking for a creative, energetic individual to join our acclaimed faculty and partake in our mission to provide high school students with a stimulating, compelling, enriching, and personally relevant educational experience. Must have previous teaching experience. Background in music and history required. Musical training desirable but not necessary."

I planed it across one-way to Indiana answering the job listing. Despite my distractions, I had miraculously picked up enough credits to earn a Masters degree. Of course I wanted to market it. I called the school, did a phone interview, and they liked what I said. They liked what they saw on paper, and apparently I was what they needed. I was hired and they flew me in. That was it.

While I was a native Midwesterner, Indianapolis seemed awfully "country" to me. The culture shock I felt was palpable, and my feet shook a bit just on landing on the soil of central Indiana. There was a truck stop I had to pass through that separated the airport from the city, which was apparently the gateway to Southern Indiana, where all "the old boys" hung. My neck prickled at that energy. Even before I entered the store, I could feel eyes upon me, following my every step as I walked through just to pick up a few things before driving into the city. I had rented a car since I was pretty sure I knew how to get into the city. The eyes, the breathing, then the voice...

"See something you need here, son?"

I bristled at the sound. "No, just the paper and this can of O.J."

He continued with his inquiry. "You just passing through, or you here from Indianapolis?"

My accent probably gave away the fact that I was a Northerner, an outsider, or an urban Black invading from the city. "Me? What do you mean?" I said. "I run things in town here, always been here. Don't you recognize me?" He was not pleased with my flippant remark. As I walked away I heard him call me a "smart sunnova bitch" under his breath. I just waved, wished him well, thanked him kindly, and left briskly.

I still had a few days before starting work, so I set up shop in the downtown area in a small apartment which put me close to the pulse of the city. This was during yet another politically tumultuous time. We had just had a party handover from the Republican double dose of Reagan, then Bush, to the Democratic Clinton party in 1993. We deserved rest from the 80's mess and this Bush. With him, there was this "read my lips" declaration that focused us on his rhetoric and not his actions.

I thought about entering the classroom again. I remembered Mrs. Anderson's words: "No matter what, joined at the hip of political action is artistic expression." I was fresh out of this Masters program doing teaching with content and cultural connect, as one friend called it. I could set up shop yet again. The Maters saved me. With plenty of strong references and letters of support, I could always get a teaching job. I remembered hating it back in Los Angeles, but it saved me from total ruin and I always had it there to keep me from sinking.

Some friends I met in Los Angeles, teachers I knew from the Masters program, told me about the Indiana system and sent me to Robert Winfrep, head of the music and arts education programs there at the Allen Arts Academy. He made me aware of the vacancy at the school, which I immediately took advantage of, and he welcomed me into the fold. Those phone conversations with Winfrep were always classic. "We need young Blacks like you to set the example, Sullivan. I'm going to help you see what you need to do to keep it all on the straight line to success."

With him, there was always an authoritative "I'm keeping the good eye on you" kind of vibe that I hated. We always clashed because I fight control freaks. They really get under my skin. They say politics is the art of compromise, but Winfrep was more an all one-sided *windbag* who was only concerned with hearing his own horn toot. I thought this was about education, not war. Nevertheless, I decided to enter the battlegrounds.

Here I was, back in the Midwest, attempting to sort it all out again. I wasn't fooling myself. My characters were trying desperately to convince me that this world was not mine to fit into, but I fought against them. I *wanted* this to work, I wanted to find what I was looking for, to settle down. In the end, they were right. The Allen Arts Academy didn't help me recover from my anxiety and paranoia, but I didn't know that yet. For the moment, I was ready for a fresh start, and I was going to fight for it.

Mr. Winfrep was the personification of Dr. Bledsoe in Ralph Ellison's *Invisible Man*. He was of Southern rearing, at least a generation older than I. He had been in the system for many years, so he had gained the respect and notoriety of those in the system, and beat the fear of the Lord into everyone else, particularly those working under his supervision. He was always dressed in a dingy suit, sloppy, ruffled, with a crumpled white shirt and a tie that was never pulled to his collar. It was as if he *couldn't* pull it up that close without choking himself. He knew there were things wrong with him and he acted full of himself to compensate. I came to understand this was a condition of his generation, and I learned to hate that. It wasn't their fault, but I couldn't help myself. I sensed he was just a political appointment, which explained much of his double talk, threats, and psyche games. Why couldn't he, particularly at this vulnerable time, just see me as good, as a plus? No, I was too new to not be suspect and it began soon after our first meeting. You see, I was ambitious, younger and I had untraditional training and ideas, but I had the credentials and the experience; I was there to teach and to reach. I could understand these kids. While I was significantly older than them, I was more like a cool, hip uncle than the grandfatherly figure projected by Winfrep. I could see I would have my ways with my students.

That first-day meeting was bizarre. In a Southern, authoritarian, slightly haughty drawl, he addressed me: "We want to welcome you here, Mr. Sullivan. You'll find our students and staff a pleasant group who are eagerly waiting to work with you. Thank you for being so patient with me over these months, but I'm a busy man, lots to do. You see this?" he asked as he pulled out a newspaper clipping with headlines honoring him as a community leader. He chirped in the third person, "Mr. Winfrep has been around shaping things in this community for many, many, many years. I know this business. I know these people and I know these kids. I know their parents, watched them all grow up around this city. We do things around here along a straight line, with efficiency, which develops results. These students are the results of our work."

I already disagreed with him and his consideration of these young adults as "results" and nothing more. I shrugged it off, attributing it simply to his proud, pointed pedagogy; I waited for him to broach the topic of why I choose the job, or what I should expect, you know, a few things that connected to me. He never really got to that.

"Let me show you our operations." He took me around, pointed through the glass doors of classrooms, saluting various students and admonishing others about taking off hats, or pressing them for their hall passes. We went into classrooms, he showed me closets and equipment, but we never got to who I was, or what I envisioned. Next, we went to my classroom, which had been abandoned by the previous teacher.

"May I ask, Mr. Winfrep, what happened to the previous instructor here?"

"Well, he didn't march. We march here and we keep a straight line straight to the results. I'm sure from all the references and the work I see you've done, you are ready to make a difference here while staying on that marching line. Did I tell you I conduct the Kalimba Singers at the university? We sing Spirituals, just the way they were meant to be done. We do the tradition, just like it had been envisioned and carried out by all the singing, conducting greats." We stop at a picture of The Fisk Jubilee singers, and it became obvious to me he was a Fisk graduate just by the gleam and glow in his face. "You see these young people? They knew the straight lines to making a better world, and they did it through their studies, the values given to them, and the straight line this music demands." He continued, "You can put your things here, and here are your room keys. I have a meeting for the next hour. We have scheduled a staff gathering in my office at noon so you can meet our folks, and they you. If you need anything else in the meanwhile, my secretary Mranda is there for your assistance."

Well, maybe this won't be so bad, I thought to myself.

Although I had been given my first marching orders and had a general understanding of the terrain, I had no map, no way to know where we were going, and I wouldn't meet my fellow soldiers until noon. As I settled into my new room and sorted through a few books left behind by the previous teacher, I thought to myself that perhaps I had found some sort of resting place, despite the promise of battles to come.

Meeting The Marching Soldiers

"Well, anytime you're ready, just let me know. Mr. Winfrep and the gang should be gathering in the conference room in a few minutes. Is there anything else I can get for you?"

Wow. Those words, the tone with which they were spoken, the sincere desire to help, and the voice sunk in and stuck to me.

This was the first official meeting of Mranda, Winfrep's administrative assistant. In my totally distracted mind, I responded, "Yes, how about an hour for lunch?" But by now I was a relatively mature and focused young professional and I was able to hold my tongue; I certainly was not going to read anything into the pleasant exchange, nor should I have. She was just being naturally professional, pleasant, and humane—and distinctively, distractingly *fine*. I politely declined her offer before hurrying back to my room to gather my notes and prepare myself for my first faculty meeting.

I walked into the conference room a few minutes before noon, hoping to run into some folks and have a chat, but they barely spoke. I must have replaced someone they liked, or displaced someone else they had hoped would get this post to get such a chilly reception. I took a moment to observe my surroundings. The conference room was very Midwestern. A few fake paintings of white people I didn't know and some dull landscapes hung on the walls around a huge twenty person conference table; at the end of the room there was an area where refreshments could be served; a components cart with a VCR, a TV, and a cassette player was tucked away in a corner.

CEDRIC'S TRUTH: THE KIDS ON STURTEVANT STREET

Soon, more people streamed in and there were all kinds of pleasant folks; then, in walked Robert Winfrep. He cleared his throat, officially calling the meeting, and everyone hurried to sit and collect themselves for a proper meeting. Winfrep started in: "Good afternoon, I'm glad, very glad to see you all here. We have quite an agenda, quite an agenda. I trust Mranda has provided you all with today's talk topics and a few of the reports from the board, who have made suggestions we'd need to implement. We saved you all some of the desserts from last night's affair, so be sure to avail yourself of the delights."

Tacky, I thought. *He is serving the board's leftovers the night before?* He went on: "Of highlight today, we have our newest faculty member, Mr. Cedric Sullivan." There were a number of agreeable hums and pleasant nods, a few claps; this was nice. He continued, "He comes to us highly trained with a Masters in American social history, with an emphasis on music and social activism. He has taught extensively in the public school system and briefly in the graduate world, and he is also a professional performing musician. Mr. Sullivan, we welcome you. Would you like to share a few words before we go around and introduce everyone to you?" I graciously accepted his welcome and said just a few courtesy words, telling them how excited I was to be there.

An older colleague flippantly asked, "What made you leave the warmth of Los Angels for Indiana? I mean," he continued without letting me answer, with a tone that stated that he wanted to start some drama, "there seems *so* much there and your work seems so *nicely* suited for teaching out there in Hollywoodland." At this point, it was hard to determine if this was a Midwestern suspicion of West coast people or if there was just a general dismissal of my work. I gave a dismissive answer, subtly ignoring the implications of his questions, instead choosing to mention the national reputation Allen Academy had gained, saying that "it seemed logical to move to a more community-centered state" where the quality of life was more consistent with the pace I wanted to work within. I got more smiles and shakes of the heads.

Winfrep chimed in. "With Mr. Sullivan's experience, we could certainly tap into this for some of our, these days, more *barren* outreach needs." He cleared his throat, then motioned for everyone to go around introducing themselves.

Here I met "the Eleven." While Winfrep headed the Visual and Performing Arts department, each faculty member there directed a smaller sub-section; some had their own subordinates and some took charge of the entire section. That day I learned their names and their departments, and I gathered my first impressions of their personalities. In the following years I would get to know them more, but my initial assumptions were for the most part spot-on.

Janice-Lee Burrows, who was from Indianapolis, headed the sculpture department and taught ceramics. She never wanted to cause trouble, but she was a quiet fire, baby, who could burn you when she wanted to. I never really knew what to make of her.

There was Jonathan Montgomery, our computer whiz and design expert. His department covered things like graphic design, photography, and later, web design. Jonathan was on the cutting edge of digital art. That computer thing I hated from the beginning, but Jonathan was a genuinely nice guy, and we eventually became very close.

There was the crusty Mr. Questions, whose name was Jack Sawyer, or, as I called him in my head, Jack-ass Sawyer. He was a local, born and raised in Indianapolis. His department dealt with traditional two-dimensional art like painting, drawing, and printmaking. He taught drawing in the most orthodox, uptight way possible, which explained his godawful personality.

Crystal Simmons, from Cincinnati, was in charge of art history and she was *fine,* herself a work of the classical masters. She had a clue about things and I liked her very much. She had a serious case of jungle fever, though—I could tell—so I couldn't do *that*, especially that close to Southern Indiana. We were nothing more than good friends.

That was the visual arts department.

Karen Singleton was from Gary. Karen taught dance, and, of course, she was my favorite. She was consistently dressed from head to toe in wrapping scarves, which seemed to pull you into her swirling orbit. She was an artist for sure.

Laura Jackson was Black and she was Proud. She directed the theater department. She always thought I was weird, which I thought was something coming from a theater person.

Next, we had Arlington Mumford, our chorale director. Arlington was an older Southern gentleman who held us up and kept us to the fires of values. I adored the man. And brother, could he cook, God! His room always smelled of cinnamon candied yams, greens, Okra, fried chicken, and muffins, making us hope he'd brought in some love straight from his iron pans. The parties he threw for some of us at his home couldn't be beat, even in Motown.

Timothy Johnston, Mr. Stay-Black, conducted the marching band, focusing on brass and percussion. He was from Atlanta, and he was all about precision and himself. He never gave us a chance to like him, with his self-absorption.

The director of the jazz band, David Bakings-Hernandez, was my salvation, a breath of fresh air. He specialized in woodwinds. I really liked him, but I never got the chance to really get to know him.

There was John Hamilton, the orchestra guy, who was the resident expert on strings. He was from Detroit. Even though he was a homeboy of sorts, he was boring, uptight, and snobby. He was an Uncle Tom, a sellout, all about pleasing his white masters. I did not like him one bit.

Susan Hamilton was John's wife, and, in the fashion of her husband, she was a female Uncle Tom. She was taught music theory and basic composition, and true to tradition, a theorist and a purist to the bone. I disliked her deeply. She hated me.

I completed the performing arts department with music history. With me, there were twelve on the team. Twelve on a mission? No, don't go there, friend.

Out of the twelve of us, there were four whites, one Asian, one Latino, two untrustworthy Uncle Toms, three die-hard "we black and we proud" people, and myself, the oddball. I only tell you this, friend, generalizing and stereotyping, because, quite honestly, race was a major factor in the ill opinions and typical exchanges that were to come. Now pour the gravy on top of that: southern, northern, education, class, ego, envy, economic intrigue, and favor tallies, and you get a pretty mess.

I won't go into any deeper detail on their personalities. Some I did misread and others were immediately on the downbeats of what I expected. You can never judge people, though, because we all wither under the scorching sun and flower after a revitalizing rain. We can only hope that our garden flowers and the weeds go away. Anyway, that was the Visual and Performing Arts division of the Allen Arts Academy. The larger school with major public and private funding took up an entire block. There was a school population of more than two thousand students. Our Eleven regularly kept company with the nearly two hundred teachers who occupied the other divisions and departments of the school. It was a massive machine, and our little gear wringers in the Visual and Performing Arts division were soiled by their worry of how the mothership structure viewed us. I never got to know the people in the rest of the school, and I didn't necessarily want to.

The Albert Allen Arts Academy had a specialized school of performing and visual arts division, a part of a larger alternative megaschool for gifted high school students. I am sure the end to my traditional teaching got its start there. It was the most palpable swirling mess of conflicting constituencies you can imagine, all gathered in one city block. I soon discovered that the teachers were divided into "us versus them" in countless configurations. The divisions fell into many different categories: it wasn't just where you got your teaching certificate, what school you attended, what region you came from, what philosophical certifications you had, what positions you held, whether you favored lecture courses or hands-on methods classes, whether you were old-school or into the new technologies—it was racial shit, too. Ah, race, our old American friend. Too many of the teachers disliked me or were suspicious of me, no matter what I did. I had arrived in hell holding a box of matches. There were fires all around and in hand. I was about to discover all of this.

Moments With Mranda

"The cool thing about musicians is they really hear shit, you know, expressive sounds in their heads." I'd tell her this, trying to sound cool without looking like I was trying too hard.

She would laugh with a deep delight it seemed. I loved her laughing. "Cedric, you so crazy around here. What are you hearing today, dear, in that head of yours?"

I had begun to develop a little problem. I'm sure it's something we all as men have to put up with. I have an eye, a fondness for the quality of beauty. This fondness would occasionally make an appearance, and I'd get distracted. My eyes, my ears, my heart, and my thinking are connected, and they respond to this beauty. I became easily distracted by Mranda, but I believed it was for all the good reasons. One has to believe in the twists and tugs of the heart, the soul; that's what draws down a great melody, right?

I read a lot of mystic poets, but of them all I was primarily a Rumi fan. I came across this poem of his:

> *There is a tradition that Muhammad said, "A wise man will listen and be led by*
>
> *a woman, while an ignorant man will not." Someone too fiercely drawn by animal*
>
> *urges lacks kindness and the gentile affections that keep men human.*

*Anger and sharp desiring are animal qualities. A
loving tenderness toward*

*women shows someone no longer pulled along by
wanting.
The core of the feminine*

*comes directly as a ray of the sun. Not the earthly
figure you hear about in*

*love songs, there's more to her mystery than that.
You might say she's not from*

the manifest world at all, but the creator of it.

Yes, I thought when I first discovered that poem. *That's me, that's what I believe.* So years later when India Arie sang, " I love a man who loves music...a man who loves art...a man who cares for spiritual things and thinks with his heart," I began to look for ladies who thought that way as well. Maybe that's what I thought I saw in her. Mranda was not young, not-so-distracted, oh-so-gracious, elegant and not-so-single. But by god, I was distracted and seduced by her deep beauty on sight. Then she spoke, smiled, and I was lost. I only got to that point because I did was I was told. I went to Winfrep's office that first day to get the information I needed from the secretary, Mranda. Her fragrance was sweet, not too strong, but distinctive, reminiscent of something my mother would wear. That sounds odd, I know, but it was familiar and made me feel like I'd come to the right place. The scent made me think of home, and that comforted me. That warm September day of 1993, she was wearing a fitted, flowing royal blue dress, paired with a deeper blue scarf. Her nails were perfectly manicured, her hair pulled back into an elegant secretary's bun. Her cat eye glasses hung from a classic rope, and her sandals exposed her delicate feet. And of course, Luther was on her CD player. Truth be told, she was a *fine* late-forties *dream*. From day one, she was nothing but incredible.

"Well, hello there, Mr. Sullivan," she said to me as she stepped from behind her desk. As if I needed more proof of her beauty or another distraction, she extended her soft hand to greet me. "We have been anxiously awaiting you. I have been reading your files over these weeks with great excitement. I feel as though I've already known you. I am so thrilled to finally get to see you person to person, soul touching soul, yes? Welcome. I trust Mr. Winfrep gave you a part of his *ordering*," she laughed respectfully. "I know you have many questions—that's why I'm here. It's my job to fill you in on everything you need to know. We have a great group of faculty and staff here, and I'm sure they will get you up to speed as well. How was your room? We've ordered a new computer, a sound system, and copier. I hope they stocked all your office gear?"

"Yes, yes," I responded distractedly, completely caught off guard. "I found the room to be really refreshing; it's got a nice open layout and there's lots of room. My goodness, I could rent it to myself and save a bundle on my apartment expenses." I had no intentions of being inappropriate or over-sharing, but it slipped out.

"Where are you renting?" she asked.

"Downtown, across from your convention arena. I know, I could have done better had I not waited to get here to search, but I was in a hurry to get out of Los Angeles."

She immediately responded, "I would have been glad to escort you around, drive you so that you could have had a wider range of choices! Are you on a long-term lease?"

At this point I was seriously distracted, sweating a bit, so I didn't want to read into the offer too much, or assume that she was being anything other than kind and welcoming. "You are so kind. I'm on a sixth month lease, so I will take you up on that offer."

While working, of course, there were many trips down to the office. There was always time to chat, ask for information, be briefed on students, transfers from other schools, setting up field trips, and, of course, to attend the weekly meetings where Winfrep dealt out his marching orders. I'd come out from those, she'd see the pain in my soul, and she would say oh-so-knowingly, "You know the saying, Cedric, there are only two energy streams: Fear and Love. You have to decide which one you swim in." She moved me. God almighty, I will never live a day when that woman's meaning doesn't bounce all within me. Winfrep, though, protected her like she was his. It wasn't so, but he pretended there was something there. I knew better.

"Winfrep," she'd say to him. "I think we have to continually recode the methods we use to represent ideas connected to new sets of values and meanings associated with images, and figures, words and symbols for our kids in this new age. Cedric's kind of work brings new symbols, new histories, new ideas and values, approaches, tactics and new paradigms, models, that inspire people to think and reason differently. I've seen what he does with our students. Education is for the civic good, not for the financial return on the investment. Be sure you tell those board members that."

One day I overheard him outside the office. "He's young and idealistic, your precious Cedric."

I heard her fire back, "Robert, I think you still see Cedric as inconsequential, but he loves you despite yourself. So when you feel the earthquakes he makes that will shake your gate, know that I told you so, old dude, and smile, then you will know."

He came out, muttered something as he walked past me, "Mr. Sullivan, on to the next, on to the next."

During those times, I became quite close with her. I became quite obsessed with her. Mranda was a champion of all the values I valued, older but not old, and I felt that in her I could find what I had been searching for. She portrayed everything I wanted for the world through her sincerity, her elegance, even just the way she moved. The times we were in didn't move like that. After many months, I had built up enough courage to invite her out, to socialize outside the work environment. I waited patiently for the right and the right moment to ask. I didn't care that I thought she might be married—that would not discourage me, nor would it deter me from stealing a few undisturbed moments with her. There was just something about Mranda that drove me crazy and at least I wanted to tell her, maybe even find out if she was drawn to me. I'm human, I couldn't help what I felt.

Eventually, I built up the nerve to very professionally ask, "Hey, Mranda, it'd be great to get a chance to have a chat sometimes, maybe grab lunch. How about it?"

To my joy she responded, "I'd love to catch up and check in on you." It seemed just perfect, safe, but then my characters had the gall to ruin my happy moment by asking, "What if someone from the school sees us with her? *Winfrep?*" I ignored them for once. Mranda and I set a time for our outing.

Before I had the courage to ask her, we had been exchanging tapes and dubbing things for each other. I had also given her a collection of Rumi poems. I knew she would love his writings. Music and poetry are the kinds of expressions that seem to carry so much about what we value in the inner places, and Mranda was deeply sensitive and appreciative of these exchanges. I began to sense from her a real closeness that went beyond the professional office pleasantries we all received from her. Winfrep sensed this as well.

For our lunch date, we chose a Thai restaurant I had seen in downtown Indianapolis, very near to where I stayed. I drove. We left the Allen Academy lot and it felt fairly natural, professional; it is perfectly normal for colleagues to go for a meal together. Was the problem just all in my mind? Had I created anxieties that weren't even necessary? I wasn't sure then, but, looking back, I bet Mranda had no fogginess in her mind and saw this simply as a chance to get away and have a pleasant meal. As soon as we pulled out of the school parking lot, my relief was palpable. I popped some great music in the car tape stereo, Luther of course, and it was very comfortable; the tension, fear, and anxiety left our space.

"Cedric, I really appreciated the Rumi, friend. And the music! That place keeps us so straight and narrow I have to have things there that bring me back to reality. And your kindness and consideration over these months has really meant a lot to me. How have you been? I know these folks have not always been so accommodating. You bring a lot of fire and they tend to be rather conservative. I hope you don't let them discourage you too much."

"No," I said, "I'm hanging in there. I get my work with my students done. Besides, I've got the committee works, the outreach projects, and I have a number of my own projects, so I'm keeping busy."

We arrived at the restaurant. On this day, it was very cold; as we ran towards the doors, the biting wind made the indoors seem a welcoming womb. It was safe. As our hostess led us to a table, I realized that this was the first social time I had had with anyone in Indianapolis, so I wondered if I could even come off as a stable person. Could I even appear stable while trying to tame the crazy obsession I had with this mature and wonderful lady, who I was sure by then was married? The waitress greeted us and we both ordered hot tea.

"Well, Mranda, how is life for you? I mean, Winfrep keeps us all in those straight lines, and you spend your whole day with him, so I can't imagine what that feels like. You've worked for him for how long?"

She pushed back from the table and sighed. "I've been working under him for the last seven or eight years, which seems like an eternity. I knew him from our church, actually. I had done some administrative secretarial work in the system before, so he asked if I would consider working as an administrative assistant when the arts and humanities division opened, and we've been there ever since. I am fond of the old bastard, but Winfrep ain't easy. I wanted to tell you the music you made for me has been a salvation."

The smile that bloomed on my face came from the deepest parts of my insides.

"I loved making those pieces for you, and I thank you too for your tapes. I have this thing in my mind about being an artist I can't shake. I'm always getting my students to try to figure out what that inner drive is, and the music, like you said, always takes it there. You made some fabulous and varied cuts! You know, Mranda, I love our exchanges because I don't really have any friends here, and our colleagues, well, they don't really get me."

She grabbed my hands and I almost lost it—my control, my mind—she looked me straight in the eyes, leaning in.

"Cedric, sweetheart, don't you even bother with those old grumpies. You just keep believing and working your thing. Your students love you because they feel what you are trying to get them to believe in. That will affect all of their work, and sooner or later it will affect your colleagues in great ways as well. As a matter of fact, I am sure it already has. Don't you think if Winfrep didn't think so he would have said something by now?"

She realized rather abruptly she was still grasping my hands, and gently let go. That set my heart pounding, and the moisture in my mouth turned to sand.

"I guess so," I said. "Speaking of Winfrep, why does he insist on this old army sergeant regimen? This is an arts academy we're talking about! And I do understand the fact that I may have to accept his bullshit, but I never have to accept it as acceptable."

"Well, Winfrep is from way, way back in the day, and I'm sure it stems from his army days, and the way they used to teach in this system, and they way they gave, or still give, merit to the old guard. You know, it's an old boys'—and I mean *old* boys—clique. But don't you worry about that. You represent a new guard and what you are bringing to the table *matters*."

I felt completely validated in so many ways. She understood, she got it, she sensed my convictions, commitments, and she knew my struggles.

"Mranda, I've known you over all these months," I began to feel confident. The sand in my mouth went away and the moisture returned. "And not once have I heard you speak of a husband or a family."

She turned away and looked out of the window. "Oh, not much to speak of, Ced."

She called me Ced.

"I have been married for many years and it's—well, it's not good, and everybody knows it. That's why you haven't heard anyone say anything. Winfrep is protective of me because he knows my husband—" I began to feel very ill. I almost regretted bringing it up. She continued. "You know, Cedric, I feel I can trust you, can't I?"

"Of course." I leaned forward and my tie went into my soup. She didn't notice. "You can tell me anything—what's going on?"

"My husband drinks constantly and he has become abusive, and I don't know what to do. There it is. I have confided in you."

I felt absolutely sick to my stomach, but I was also thrilled. Of course it was a terrible thing to feel happiness at such a sickening confession, but it meant that she wasn't emotionally involved with someone else. It meant I might have the tiniest of chances with her.

"You see, that Rumi you gave me a while ago confirmed that I have been married to someone who is not my soulmate—I sense this gap in my life, and that poem stated it so clearly and oh-so-meaningfully. Cedric, it ripped through me at each read. I haven't been the same since you gave it to me, and I have been looking for a way to say *thank you*."

What I took away from that conversation is that you never know what's going on with people. Secondly, I began to wonder if I'd been wishing for something I wasn't ready to handle. Life is always throwing surprises at you, and sometimes they catch you unawares. Where was this all going?

I took a deep breath and said, "I'm here to hear." Our conversation spilled well over the lunch hour, and before we knew it, two hours had gone by. *Good thing I have a free period after lunch*, I thought. Of course, Winfrep was waiting at the door when we returned. Great.

"So, y'all were expecting to extend your lunch right into dinner time, huh?"

That was my first of many infractions against the marching orders of Mr. Winfrep. Mranda just laughed and said, "Did you take my messages for me, Robert? Did you put out any of your own fires while we were away?" She was completely unflustered by his schoolmarmish way. She knew him well, so she could laugh it off. I, though, would certainly suffer greater scorn and consequences. I didn't know at the time quite what to make of this experience, but it delivered me into a better place with Mranda, a closer space, despite the heat I got from then on from Winfrep. I saw Mranda many more times.

Loss and Discovery

"Please don't talk so loudly, I can't hear the voices in my head."

I remember that sign was posted on a beachside café I frequented. That would be me. I had to give space to those characters wrestling in my soul for my head's attention. We all must be guided, right?

While my time at the Allen Academy was a stressful succession of professional battles, I suffered greater losses. My pain was increased and my soils became more disrupted. I became dislodged from life due to the loss of both of my parents. Well into their seventies, their breaths, which worked as well as a well-oiled clock, never needing winding, stopped. They had always been there for me. All my running, all my reaching for my dreams, they were there, extending the ropes when I reached my wit's ends. It was soon after I relocated to the Midwest that I heard the news that they had both expired. Dead within days of each other. One stopped, and a few days later, the other followed. It was as if sound and air disappeared and my insides stopped working. They were gone. I was numb with disbelief. I rushed home. How can you make sense of such a tragedy?

In some ways, that was better. How can you qualify a better death? Well, if you attached death to a quality of a kind of peace, and if you add to that lived a good life, you touched many lives, and you are blessed to pass away in peace… that helps the pain. At least that's the story I tell myself each day. I had to drive to Detroit for their funerals, which I try to block out, but...

During this time, I found a master teacher whom my father had known before he passed: Harold Cruse, the great teacher and unorthodox scholar. Driving between Indianapolis and Detroit, I stopped at Ann Arbor, Michigan, where Harold ran a humanities lecture series at the university. I discovered his local stomping grounds, and I frequently attended his lectures. Sometimes, I would meet the great mind at a local café where I was told he would gather students for afternoon talks, which were legendary on the campus. This street, which ran through the center of campus, was lined with streams of shops, ice cream and treats specialty stores, coffee houses, and university stores where you would buy books and university merchandise.

Like most college towns, Ann Arbor was monied, bankrolled by the presence of the university, and this street was its crown strip. There, at Simon's Café, Cruse would talk about politics and culture, Black people, gender, American whiteness and its effect on Black determination or the lack thereof. He could be seen walking with a slow, determined pace, cane in hand, pipe in mouth, a newspaper clutched under his arm. He always headed toward his local spot on the strip. After several visits to see him, he and I became friends. We talked about everything and more.

The ultimate happened one day. All the students had gone, and we sat there in Simon's drinking his favored cup of black coffee—like my mom, no sugar with half and half. He asked me, "Cedric, I have appreciated our talks. You have a lot of wonderful ideas; why not come and share some in my classroom? I think my students would enjoy having you around." I couldn't believe it. After that, I'd shoot from Indianapolis to Ann Arbor whenever I could to join Professor Cruse in class. I watched. I listened. I took meticulous notes, and I tried to internalize his methods and his musings. What impacted me was his notion of artistic responsibility. He'd fuss, "It remains for the Negro intellectual to create his own philosophy and bring the facts of the cultural history in focus with the cultural practices of the present." In advanced societies, he would argue, the role of the artist was to create new ideas, new images of life. He said ideas must not be "subordinated to the whims and desires of politicians, race leaders, or civil rights entrepreneurs."

CEDRIC'S TRUTH: THE KIDS ON STURTEVANT STREET

Everybody I ran into over the years I began to see as the obstacles to the world I yearned to create. Cruse believed that the creative Black person must take seriously the ideas that culture and art belonged to people and pursue, with all the revolutionary implications, that idea. That became my religion. This was what I was pushing all doors to walk in and make the room into. That's what got me into trouble, too. He'd pull my ear to his lips and whisper, "Cedric, man never holds up his end of the deal. His great accomplishments are of naught because he undermines them with cruelty and greed, which are inwardly self destructive. Cedric, to explore, seeking truth is important. But it is more important to tell the truth you find as you seek it. Don't hide from it as you are finding it. Don't hide from it. But don't go crazy with it either!"

During those lectures, I'd sit there, intently listening, with these much younger college kids. They never got it. I got him, and I loved him. He was so grand and so messy, always dressed in a vest, worn over a crumpled, dingy white dress shirt and baggy pants, with scuffed-up brown wing-tipped shoes. From his neck hung a homemade rope made of shoes laces and rubber bands that held up the glasses he wore, which were mended across the bridge with tape. He would pace the floors in front of the students, looking up gently and gingerly pontificating about the meaning of the soul, and what a commitment to history and culture really meant. He was the kind of tender, thoughtful gentleman you imagined having long talks with and getting counseled by on an evening stroll.

I made sure I remembered every line, committed to it. "How you deliver the truth, how it connects is what counts. But don't get crazy with it." What did he mean? He was like my mother, always mixing and matching sayings, but I got it. I stayed on it. It was Cruse who taught me how to live out the ideas of the intellectual matters, then internalize these and walk them without preaching them. I gained that from him. He was the quintessential example of the non-gowned scholar, the non-degreed man of letters and ideas of the mind. He was my model and I loved him. When he passed away a few years ago, I felt like I'd lost another parent. I didn't attend his funeral. I couldn't bear that much loss in my world.

Tension Mounting

Imagine getting stabbed all over by dozens of knives, all day, every day. The pain saturates the walls of your interior, cutting deep, tearing you apart day by day. You plaster a smile on your face, but the rabid butterflies in your stomach are rioting against some type of heartburn, the forces in your body clashing and making you ill.

That's a terrible feeling. A cloud settles over you, depressing you. Who can feel creative and free in that? Who can feel human there? That's how I felt at the Allen Academy.

"Well, Cedric, your students seem to really be responding to your classes. You must feel very good about that, I'm sure." Her words and sneers she always tried to pass off as collegially critical. She'd come into the faculty conference room, where I'd stop in to have a word with the computer guy, Jonathan. Susan Hamilton was the evil She-Tom whom I disliked fiercely. She always dressed too tightly. I answered her back cooly and unflustered. "Why, thank you, Susan. I'd like to think they're learning, and glad to hear they are enjoying it, too."

She pushed harder. "In one of your assignments, as I saw, you dismissed the need for harmonic analysis, preferring, as you call it, *creative listening*, where they invent stories that allow them to, uh, *see* the music? What exactly are they *seeing*?" She spat the word "seeing" with blatant sarcasm. You know the sound of a smart-ass? She exemplified it. She envied my work. I guess she hadn't heard that this was *my* class and *my* assignment, but I played along anyway. "Well, Susan, I simply want the students to hear music in connection with their other imaginative senses, trying to get them to see it as an expression of their experiences, not as an execution of set rules."

She snipped back, "Yes, but this is *music*, Cedric, not painting or dance. We don't imagine anything without a structure to work within. I mean it's not jazz improvisation, or rock and roll—it's music, right?" She implied with her tone that jazz and rock weren't actually music, and I was a bit offended. See, I have no love for rules when they obstruct creative flow, and she was one major obstruction and a pain in the ass, big time, always pounding on my attempts to free these kids up. My God, they were kids, not soldiers! She never understood me, and I never had any love for her. I tried to reason with her anyways.

"Susan, I know you smile and grin and bear it, but deeper underneath there is a twisted vein of discomfort and suspicion of me for some reason, and I'm not aware of its origins. Our interactions will play out as suspect, full of resentment-based word and eye play, which is toxic and dangerous."

She countered in her dismissive way, "There is nothing *toxic* here, *Cedric*, and I'm no danger to you, or you me. I just think you have ideas that need some running through. That's it."

I finished my first full year at Allen Academy with that kind of bullshit on my plate. I was always trying and being made to feel that my first job was to prove myself, my worth to the others. Year two was not good either. I was approaching my first third-year review, and I did not feel good about it. Although my work with the students was great and gratifying, the very air of that institution choked me and the sprit of my work, my ideas. The spirit and tension of unresolved resentment, professional frustration, painted loudly the exterior frames of every exchange we had, by word, written memos, and eyeball to eyeball glances.

The war of ideas was on! In one of those classic Winfrep Tuesday meetings, the air was tight; I could feel battles brewing beneath the surface of the fake Midwestern pleasantries. There they were, the soldiers of mediocrity, meanness and mania: Jack-ass Sawyer, John the

Uncle Tom, his wife, the She-Tom, Tim "True Black" Johnston, and Laura "Stay Black" Jackson. We sat there as Winfrep raised the combative idea of staying on the straight line, true to his marching orders and their reigning philosophy and pedagogy.

I raised, with no intention of pointing fingers at anybody, the issue of where we were going to recruit new students from in the coming years. How were we going to interest younger kids to choose the arts or writing, instead of heeding the call of principal headmasters and curriculum crashers up on the big block who were headstrong fastened on score testing, and job core, joining the Army, and the other madnesses they were pushing at the students in those days?

I stood convicted on the idea of us being focused and on new downbeats, at least talking about where we might be going, but Winfrep needed to back me up. I told them, "In an institutional framework, our motion can only be affected by sound leadership, and that leadership must be grounded with vision, driven by the mission, a timed plan with implementation and mechanized actions toward good results, and always anchored in integrity. Kids are drawn to that kind of positive focused energy."

Winfrep led the fueling of the fires. "Cedric, are you saying our results have never been a beacon of any good measurement that has shaped our curriculum, teaching, and development over the years? That's leadership too. I think our straight line has been pretty well and consistently drawn."

"Oh, no," I tried to clarify. "I just meant there needs to be more consensus among a constituency that values a philosophy and is committed to a plan."

Jack-ass interjected, "I have to ask, Cedric. I mean, I've been teaching here for a while and I think our philosophy has been well-tuned and has created results, don't you think?" It always started out this way. Jack-ass never gave up on watering the seeds of doubt he had planted in others' minds. I was always painted as the bad guy.

Then the unpredictable Janice-Lee stepped in the water. "I'm with Cedric on this one. We spend too much time arguing in disarray, without the benefit of trying to make sure we iron out some of these differing approaches. The heard, projected voice has to be at least publicly on one accord that's come together, because we at least show we care about the things we say we want to be committed to. It takes time to sit and engage with each other. The kids can read our divisions, you know. We shouldn't be proud of that, it's not good." She was actually helpful that time.

Immediately after, Susan Hamilton began spouting her crap. I sat there wishing I could push the eject button on this heifer. She started in her usual way, trying to sound collegial, but you could clearly see the drool slowly dripping from her teeth, down the side, out of her mouth, and down her neck. "Our ideas can't be so singularly driven, hot-headed either, prone to emotive and unreasonable outbursts. Cedric, I just see this as another way we can't ever move on." I wasn't ever emotional as much as I was passionate about my points. Why were they so uptight about everything?

Uncle John, whose ideas were never original, echoed his wife. "We should always be driven and grounded by a more sensible approach tied to upholding the directions of the whole group."

Arlington saved me, not for the first time, and brought some balance. "You know, you have to raise a consistent and courageous voice of consciousness sometimes to combat any form of divisiveness. Malice always disrupts the potential spirit for people to be in community with one another. I think Cedric raises a good idea for us to at least consider. Change and redress aren't always so bad, you know."

It took a lot of courage and drew all my energy to speak up and be in battle mode all the time, but it had to be done. Somebody needed to do it. My characters pushed me to be vocal.

I knew personally I had a well-tuned, well-organized, and well-oiled mind well-suited for what I needed to do, but unfortunately, I lacked mechanism for doing it in an orderly fashion. Details just got slippery with me. Winfrep held this against me, but hey, I'm an artist, not an accountant.

I know now that losing my parents added to an already-worsening situation at Allen Academy. My job, well, that thing was suffocating me. I, friend, was caught in the Matrix, and my exchanges with those faculty members over the months were horrible. They were caught in the Matrix, too. There was dedication and these were very gifted and efficient educators, but I just didn't fit in with them in total. They as a body never came to trust me, and Winfrep played that up. The divisiveness of his favoritism, silences, and threats didn't allow me to find a consistency of camaraderie to trust because there were so many other things in the mix.

He closed us down. "Well, then. I think we're always on the right road, Arlington, staff, it's ok for us to visit the victories, the vicissitudes, and the valleys too. I agree. Good meeting, all. I'll have Mranda type these up and we'll have these in some kind of meaningful form soon. We'll continue later. Now, I think you all have classes, right?"

This always seemed silly to me. We were the high school teachers, not the high school students. He in his mad, schoolmarmish way extolled, "March on, we must make the mark." The others left, Winfrep leading the soldiers out.

Thank God for Crystal, David, Arlington, and the silent one, Jonathan. In those days as I marched toward my ruin, I floated from meeting to meeting without knowing what the agenda was, why it was being served that day, and who was going to take the first bite out of me. I was marked. Usually, everybody left quickly after the meetings. One dark, rainy day, which seemed to symbolize all I was going through, I remained at the conference table with Jonathan. I sipped my by-then cold coffee while he typed away on that box which was his constant companion. Jonathan foresaw the reign of technology as well as my demise. I decided to confide in him.

"Jon, bro. Do you ever feel deceived, absolutely stabbed in the back, over and over, publicly, again and again?"

He didn't even look up to respond. "With you and company I can see the dagger going into your flesh, and I can see and feel your blueish green blood spilling out, my burden-laden brother." We laughed out loud, but inside I cried with my characters.

"Come on, you know." I wanted someone to hear this. "You see their twisted smiles. I feel the heat, it's all in slow motion. I can feel the heat inside me all day before I even walk in here."

CEDRIC'S TRUTH: THE KIDS ON STURTEVANT STREET

Jon was always one for drama when you encouraged him. He went into this thing, a kind of fake British commentary voice you might hear on the BBC. "Now I see it, the bloody bastards. Camera pans out, shows everyone in the room. You don't see it? I do. They are all smiling, all with knives drawn and pointed at you at once, sitting there pretending to be oblivious to the attack you're under."

I let out a sad chuckle before going on. "Jon, I'm in that place, like Neo from the Matrix. While they are setting me up to take the Red pill, I take the Blue one instead, hoping to release myself into the truth, removing Morpheus' splinter." We cracked up, a pair of sci-fi-loving geeks. I asked, "Jon, bro, remember those lines?

"You felt it your entire life. That there's something wrong with the world. You don't know what it is, but it's there. Like a splinter in your mind - driving you mad... It is the world that has been pulled over your eyes to blind you from the truth." We marked that rainy day with a laughter despite the menacing Winfrep minions who had minutes ago been ready to eat me alive.

I escaped that day, but they continued to spin their webs, waiting for me to get stuck so they could devour me. Eventually, I fell into their traps, I caved in, my strength was zapped, my morale minimized. I fell into regular fits of depression. I heard more voices, sometimes telling me different things. I was paranoid and saw and heard everyone coming at me. Migraines pained me for over a year. They were like hot bands of intense heat that accompanied every thought in my head. It hurt to think, to reason, so I was left with nothing but my voices, which spoke more often to me and advised me. The doctors said it was stress. I had to figure it out or I would have had a stroke.

It was Mranda who allowed me to escape through the joys of pleasant conversation, talks that touched down and landed in places that brought me no attacks, harm, humiliation, or stress. I would be in her office constantly, wishing I could be in her arms as well. I became more obsessed with just hearing her comforts whenever I could. "Cedric, how many times have I told you to just forget them, love?" She'd say that occasionally, but I'd be hoping and longing more each time she'd say it.

"Forget the fuss and feud with them, and stay with your kids. They love you, Ced." Did she know? Delighted with her new discovery, she said, "Wow, where do I keep getting that from? I like that for you, it's cute. Ced. Hmm. Anybody else ever call you that? I bet your mom called you Ced, didn't she?"

Well, I thought, *no, not Mom,* but it did move something inside. It didn't mater, though, she could have called me Cryboc and it would have been just fine. I needed her any way and all the time I could get. I would take whatever she had to share with me. "Cedric, isn't it interesting that those who have the most to share end up being the ones the world is most willing to silence and shut down? You be on the side of the good-willed, you'll be just fine." She was not only my best friend, but she also became my medicine. I reveled in her presence.

New Calling Brewing

"You're an artist-revolutionary. You will lead people to remove the splinters from their minds, their ears, their hearts. The greedy bureaucracy blinds us all, and art will restore our senses. This is your mission, but watch out for the detractors."

My characters told me this, and I began to see it as the reality. I was on the right track. I knew what they were talking about, 'cause the detractors weren't being subtle at all. John Hamilton, the orchestra director from Detroit, was never supportive, always adamant in his dislike for anything outside the box. His wife was as much of an Uncle Tom as him, but at least she was willing to experiment, even though she always colored inside the lines. She pushed boundaries all the time, but she needed a rule to follow. She, unlike myself, was a theorist and lived and died by the rules. Our disagreements were typically around aesthetic issues, what was hip and what was not edgy enough, how students should be trained to value different kinds of music. We clashed all the time, even simply passing each other in the hallway. One particular day, Jonathan and I were leaving for lunch. I remember it well because it was a happy day. Jonathan had received yet another new computer that week, and I had been heavily and happily immersed in some new song. We were seemingly floating down the hall through a wave of high-spirited students, some at their lockers, some running down the hall.

"Slow that down, young man. This is not a racetrack, son. I know your mother, and she did *not* bring you up in a barn!"

Winfrep's drawl sounded odd against the X Generation's hip hop-infused banter.

The She-Tom came over to us.

"You two! I can't tell you all from the students. You mix right in with them."

"No, *they* can tell the difference, they know who we are. See, Susan, it's our spirits doll, we are young at heart, and our minds are in the right directions. That's all." We laughed, amused with ourselves. I loved watching her slow boil; you could see the red in her veins and smell the smoke before it started coming out her nostrils.

"You may be young at heart," she shot back, "but I sure hope they don't follow the example you try to set for them, otherwise they're never going to get their acts together. These kids are lost in all their distractions. You know what Winfrep says, shoot for the straight line. They'll get it. Even from the two of you." She laughed as if we were funny. At that moment, she really deserved to be called a bitch. I'm not sorry.

"Well, Cedric," Jon spoke up, trying to diffuse the tension, "we just live in the belly of the beast to heal the institutional wounds from the inside, meet the good workers, the gold miners who work inside the machine." That was it, but it said everything. Jonathan was always quite reserved; it was difficult to get him to stand up for anything. He was never as flustered with them as I was. Most of our meetings would find him bathing in the glow of a computer screen. Winfrep had a few at the table and allowed us to use them in our meetings, way before laptops. The others, Crystal, Karen, Arlington, Tim, Laura, Janice-Lee, Jack, and David used these meeting times to fight among themselves, mostly about sharing students. Everybody wanted the star pupils in a competitive arts education environment, largely because Winfrep held them to it. It was about results. When the results were largely shown by student performance, educators wanted to the show off these students, especially in ensembles. Inevitably, the teachers fought over which talented individuals would represent their departments.

I would have preferred to focus on discussing the implementation of a more qualitative approach to teaching, correcting critical thinking issues, how these students saw their creative ideas connecting to the world. In the classroom, I tended to put an emphasis on getting them thinking beyond where they were from, what they were doing at this moment, and rather focusing on where they were headed.

One day in class we went at it. One of the students asked, trying to pull me into a snare as they sometimes would do, "Mr. Sullivan, what difference does freedom of speech make if the artist is regulated to only say what's for the common good? What if I want to say what I want?" He knew this would get me.

"Well," I started out. "One of the functions of art is to help us listen better to the world we live in. You *have* to listen to the world. I don't really advocate free artists' expression because freedom is ultimately our biggest enslavement." That would rip 'em. I paused for a moment to let them absorb that. "Without responsibility or accountability, an artist will be confined to satisfying just his own needs, which serves very few, really. What the public thinks, how they respond is what at the end of the day you'd want reflected. The artist's message can only spread through the public's interpretation, so the artist needs to be aware of the public's particularities."

"Who has the time, Mr. Sullivan? Everybody's pulling you their way. I want my work, what I'm down with to stand for *me*, and in the end that serves a lot of people too, if I'm doing what I'm supposed to be doing, which is finding my truth, as you say, right?"

Now *that* was thinking, and I didn't mind that it didn't agree with my views, because it meant the students were thinking independently. That's what mattered to me. I cared that I was preparing them to go out into the world, not so much how many tricks they could learn while we were with them.

You can see I defined our mission differently. Of course this always got me in trouble, this marching out of line. A whole pack of these so-called colleagues were locked into regional provincialisms, the gate-keeper standards, and they spurned my perspectives and initiatives as an outsiders' unneeded action and take on more national, global views, which were "beyond the mission." Even then I felt committed to the teaching. A few of us who were eager to push the students were seen as going outside of the range of activities, core methods, and approved approaches that were being taught by the old-guard Indianapolitans.

For example, I had developed a regular visiting relationship with the modern arts museum director, Lori Gauss. I planned to take my music history classes to the art museum. I simply believed that education needed to be extended to experiences outside of the classroom. I'd plan this out within our budget and concoct a plan to present to the department. The idea was that students should see broader definitions of artistry, what lines, texture, color, and a juxtaposition of themes and forms related to expression could do; how these compositions connected to the ways we in society have to consider a balance of ideas, and how these themes related to social balances, justice, rebellion, and peace.

Tim started to question me at every chance about this initiative. Like I told you, he was a marching band guy: sharp, loud, and brassy. For him, everything and everyone had to be in perfect formation on the pre-existing dots, and everything he saw was split into Black and not Black enough.

"What does that say to our children, man? Art museums?! Nothing but the white man's imagery. The white man's history. Dig that? *His*-story. Not ours."

I'd try and help this brother out, but he was too lost in the lost era, the sixties, thinking we were still in a revolution that wasn't going to be televised.

"Cedric, take them to the Afro-American Marches History Museum up on Broadway Street, man. That's where they gonna learn some real deep, teaching-tooling stuff they can use, my brother."

I'd try to appeal to the greater good, but it was a lost cause. I'd try and explain, "The museum is one of my favorite places in the world! For me, those objects represent artistic energy meant to connect with and record human experiences. That applies to *all* of us."

Then the She-Tom would chime in. "What connections between musical thinkers can you make? Can you at least stretch a bit here with me, Cedric? Gershwin, Stravinsky, Schoenberg, Miles Davis. They dealt with art and form, yes, but how does that connect to what's in the museum? Why not wait until there is a more relevant showing?"

They would never let me be, and my characters warned me of their attempts to singe my soul and de-program my student soldiers.

I ignored the naysayers and planned a trip with Lori anyways. Lori Gauss was a very directed, energetic, and pleasant woman who dressed with incredible detail. She was a piece. I often told her there should be an exhibit just to show her taste in fashion. She was sharp all the time. Her mind was wide as the sky, too, and she loved to open young people up. I would learn more about the world we wanted by just listening to her speak to my students. "What I want most for you all do to is to keep in mind the power of cultural history. Ask yourselves what it preserves, what it projects, and how it penetrates identity, in both good and bad ways. When you consider that, how does the piece change?" The students' eyes would just beam with wonder. Once she had them, she'd go on. "We here believe museums are transformative places. I want you to think through several interpretive lenses about the way these pieces, paintings, and artifacts frame human experience and expression. I want you to think not so much about just history, or as they say, *his*-story, but about other stories and our-story. How would you paint or sculpt history, what questions would you ask? Now, without reading the descriptive plates, what questions, experiences do you think the artist was thinking about? Then," she would draw out the word for dramatic effect, "before you go too far in your own mind," this she said with such excitement that kept even the most solemn of us on edge, "I want you to immediately read the title of the piece and its short descriptive narrative. What I want to do is get you to sharpen your own read and interpretive languages as you define how you feel about what you see, and see how much of your sense of that expression comes close to the artist's original intent. Then, let's take notes and talk about what you discovered."

That explanation, that push to probe, deepened my students' understanding of reception of images and stories, and their own inquiry. It made them deeper thinkers. In this exchange I also had an opportunity to be deliberate about broadening their pictures of the world, using that space to link them with meaningful explorations that challenged them to connect more powerfully. It made a difference, I could see it after every trip. Lori and her staff were particularly helpful in engaging in these questions, searching for interesting objects with stories, making connections to their collections, to the larger world, and cementing a pedagogy I would use for everything I did related to art, appreciating its ability to lift the critical questions about human experiences to be celebrated and lived through. As she would say so many times, "It's as if every time we encounter these pieces, these expressions, we expanded our reach towards a truth in some way." That made a tremendous impact on my students. I just translated that into a philosophy that infuriated my detractors, the haters, because they weren't willing to stretch, and become better. They were keeping truth locked in empty ideas and boxes. I wasn't going to stay around in lockdown mode.

Up Against The Wall

The struggle against power, the angst that overwhelms you in trying desperately to define yourself, is huge.

I had both Black and white students, as well as a fair number of Asian and Hispanic kids. Our students of color and ethnicity had a different conversation of reckoning going on in their eyes when viewing some pieces and hearing "the rule of the white world." I learned quickly as a teacher how to wrestle with this disparity.

Even this abstract way of revealing universals, perspectives from other angles—as bodies, lines, shapes, modes of expression, color reconfigured—allowed these young people to see that nobody set that frame but the creator, or that the frame was more flexible than we were led to be believe. My students began to make that leap into another order of consciousness by thinking openly as creative agents. Art immersion always had that kind of reordering power over my mind, and it was what I tried to relate to these students. Identities are shaped by the realization that creative cultural production contradicts ideas of normalcy; it demands new definitions of normalcy. I would repeat these words to myself in the mirror.

I began to think I had students in my classes who were spies and reported that I was somehow leading an ideas insurrection against the Allen Academy codes for normalcy. My characters warned me of these spies. I'd return to the school and, sure enough, one of the music heads would condescendingly say, "What did you all discover in your class today?" like some kind of small-minded put down. I would always snap back, "Many worlds of meanings, my dear colleague, many worlds of meanings."

Although Winfrep gave me the monetary support for the buses, the expense of the trip, and the time off on afternoons for such excursions, he always complained in the meetings that too much of this kind of thing distracted students from the straight line. The traditional folks saw a modern museum as a waste where no art could be seen; the musicians, hardcore purists, saw this a wussy activity, and the hardcore "Black pride" guys thought the museum was another example of racism and forced Eurocentrism in the curriculum, consistently insisting we go to the Afro-American Museum. Of course there were others who saw this all outside of the board's mission statement for the academy and argued that the best experience was a focused classroom environment where students had to have unbroken contact with teachers, considering the already-hectic schedules and the back-and-forth traipsing between the buildings the students already had to do.

All it took to cast some Blues and chaos was four of them, even though my other colleagues recognized the tremendous value in such work. I wanted my kids to see the world out there and to be felt, though. Many of these kids' parents had no time, money, or interest to invest in art exhibits, so I argued that it was our job to extend and expand the experiential; that was our task and challenge as educators.

But friend, the more touchy-feely, philosophical I was perceived to be, the more many of my colleagues got stuck in their ruts. Lots of tension aired around that because they felt if you were thinking forward, you were moving too fast, or had your head too high in the sky. Suspicion became a block to my colleagues being open to my ideas. This was big for them. Over the course of six years, they began to sit on high perches, like vultures, swooping down on everything dead or alive they thought they could eat. This blinded them and crusted their hearts. We battled over everything. There were race issues, what was Black or not, what was pedagogically sound, what the board wanted, how much this cost, how unorthodox we looked to the larger school, class contact time, schedule and room rehearsal conflicts, music skills for performance or life skills for living, business ideas versus artist ideas and expression. Most importantly, who got to show off the students as the example of their great teaching? Did I mention anything about what the students wanted, or what their benefits might be? You get my point.

I saw our opportunity as a way to show the value of arts in preparing students as culture-citizens who could fully go out and be professional people impacting our society. My colleagues saw this opportunity as a way they could highlight their own achievements through their students' performances. The board would be pleased and the larger division would allocate more money for more programming, office equipment, instruments, and lab tech support, and studio and concert hall renovations. This went on and on. But someone arguing for the values and the benefit of student education, what it does for the lives and the potential impact in the world? All that seemed like voodoo magic or something equally distasteful to that group. And while people would nod their heads in agreement to the value pieces, at the end of the day it was all about how many board members showed up at the concerts.

We all got the cash side—got to keep lights on—but the cultivation of the inner cultural side of this always rang truest for me. Personality conflicts, mistrust, and such continued to be a part of our daily interactions.

"Mr. Sullivan." Uh-oh. When I was in for it, he'd start this way. I knew this time it had been Winfrep himself who had noticed something. "Your colleagues and I at Allen Academy have been concerned that the ideas you seem to hold on to so passionately are keeping you, and maybe your students, from all you have the talent to get us to, Cedric." I never really got what he wanted me or anyone else to do in this regard. Where were we supposed to be going, where was I supposed to be taking them? He droned on. "Now, no question, you are a talented instructor, but it's your politics that poison you, son. Do you hear yourself?"

Am I hearing myself!? I was born hearing myself, you old bastard! I thought and wished I could say to him. I hated Winfrep more and more each day, and so did all my characters. "What politics are you speaking of, Mr. Winfrep?" He'd always point in the direction of his office, motioning for me to meet him there, he being two steps behind me like I was being marched down to the headmaster's personal lion's den to be devoured. After we got in the office, he shut the door behind us and sat down. He stared at me, clumsily knocking over his music educator's coffee cup filled with pens. He crossed his hands over the tired pile of reports he was so devoted to.

"Now tell me again, son, what is it with you?"

I began yet again. "I just see things differently, that's all, Mr. Winfrep."

"You make it difficult on yourself, son. Why not just stay on the clear paths, till you get to higher grounds, so you can see where you come from, before you start in on where ya going, Cedric?"

"Well, I have discovered in my own research a cyclical relationship between being Black and being American. Rock, folk, Black underground movements, Beat poets and the avant-garde, Coltrane-Ayler to Warhol-Velvet Underground, social criticism and hip hop are all anti-commercial-establishment and inextricably bound, and the kids love this! They are learning so much. Teaching them about it how we can fix it." Now that I think back, I shouldn't have said the "anti-establishment." That was a sure trigger.

"*Fix* this?" He couldn't believe me. "What do you think needs *fixing*, Cedric? Do you have to be wound up so tightly, son?" Arrrrghhh, that old Southern *stuck* generational thing. I refrained from snapping back, but I didn't have to in my mind: "Wake up, Winfrep! Wake up, Allen Academy! Wake up, world!"

I became even deeper, darker in my ways of thinking about this and I was convinced, still am, that the world was deaf and blind and couldn't dance to the right beat. I was a new beats maker. I taught those kids to be concerned with racism, sexism, and the living issues of the under-classed: unemployment, housing, police brutality. Of course the current wave of this critique-protest was carried by punk and rap, which were huge for our kids. And while this seems obvious, what's of note is that revolutions continue to erupt, new expressions of social dissatisfaction. Then there are more reactions against that, new forms arise and it's always done, mechanized by musicians and artists. Ultimately what always happens is the industry co-opts that energy, markets it and sells it as theirs. The corporates! We can eliminate them and their practices when we band together. I could lead this!

"Music means more than music," I would pound on the table. And did this get a rise from Winfrep and those in our meetings over these years? Yes! "Mr Winfrep," I went on. "We can't speak about the spiritual or historical significance of things before we confront the humanity, or search for humanity, which only grows from these social realities." I would become as a possessed preacher in those meetings. And looking back now, I can see how some of those stiffs on our staff never got with this sort of thing and never got me either.

Cedric, Can I Come Over?

"Cedric, I need you to meet me somewhere. I need to speak with you— better yet, can I come over?"

The call came one blistery cold evening. Her voice shocked me as it pleased and warmed through the phone.

"Sure, Mranda, come on over. Are you OK? Is everything alright?"

"I'm fine, but I have to get out of here, and I wanted to talk with you. See you in about thirty?"

" Why of course" I said.

"Goodbye Cedric."

She hung up the phone. I fell back on my couch, sunk in, man! What was it, what did she need to say to me? I got myself together, cleaned up a bit and rummaged through the cabinets and fridge to be sure I had something to offer her to drink, or snack on. It was 9pm on a Sunday evening, a highly unusual time to receive a call from her at home. Never mind that she was coming out to downtown. She lived out in suburban-land. Man, this was serious, and I began to get nervous. Could her husband have been beating her now, again? Was he going to follow her to where I was? Did he know about our times together?

What music would I put on?

If I put on some Luther Vandross, too hot, boy, no way.

If I put on classical, no, too impersonal.

If I put on some jazz, no that's too active.

If I put on hip hop, hell, no!

If I put on some Keith Jarrett trio? Yes!
And some hot coffee.
Just right.

There are no flowers in here…yikes! OK, let a little air in here, it should smell naturally refreshed, not like freshly sprayed air deodorant. Light, yes. I have to have it lit so she doesn't think I'm trying to catch her in her vulnerability. Where will we sit? Across from each other, next to? Oh God, those silent, uncomfortable "should I kiss her?" moments…

I caught my breath and put on Mom's contemplative concoction, a cup of hot coffee. Then I just sat and waited for Mranda to come over. Thirty minutes stretched to one hour, then the buzz. I took a deep breath to calm myself, then I walked to the door.

I opened the door, and in that fleeting moment it was as if the pieces were falling into place, the pieces I had waited and hoped for. I had clarity. It felt like warm air whooshing in, and her fragrance; my heart was racing with excitement. Her presence in that surreal second was like oxygen. Her light shone forth; we would make a plan, I'd help her. I could stay here in Indianapolis, I thought, I just needed that light and that anchor in my life, that inspiring spirit, this answer to a prayer—and I don't even pray—and she was now truly walking into my life. I stood there with my arms outstretched, welcoming the warm embrace I was to receive, that comfort, this woman.

Then the warm air cooled and the lights dimmed, then went out.

"Cedric, I have to leave here. I can't live with this monster anymore, so I have to leave town. I'm going to stay with my sister in Seattle, way out West where I can escape this hell I'm in. I'm so sorry. You have been such a light in my life. I just wanted to come and tell you this before I left. Winfrep and the gang, well, he needs something to do, Cedric, it's long overdue. He'll have to run his own ship for a minute until they find a temp, I guess. The faculty, you all are tremendous, dedicated; you'll be alright.

"As to you my friend, you'll be just fine. I will always be here for you, but now I've got to run to figure this out, it's the only way. Spirit to spirit? I've got to go now, Cedric —thank you."

She never sat. We had no conversation. She never sipped the warm coffee with me. She just kissed me on the cheek, touched my forehead with that soft hand, and hurried down the hall, back onto the elevator, and out of my life.

Let Me Out Of Here!

"Cedric, you can always tell when people are wrong, because they don't do the right thing." I could hear her lovely words in my soul's ear, coming in as instruction through this maze after she had gone.

I could remember her last rants back at Winfrep. "I'm sorry, this is a bunch of drama that doesn't even add up to a Saturday afternoon matinee."

"Look, Cedric, at who's complaining," she would say, "and then look at who's contributing. There is your dividing line between your failures and your successes." She was my protective angel, and now she was gone. After Mranda left, things for me went from bad to worse. I think they thought I put ideas of leaving in her head. They were on the attack and I never saw it coming. I would sit there in meetings and watch these vultures swipe at my integrity, claim not to hear my ideas, invalidate my work and successes over and over again. They would steal the ideas that I presented in debates or confrontations. Then they would lie on me and take things I had said out of context to paint me as some kind of crusader against the causes. You know, I'd rather be hated for what I believe in and who I am than to be held in somebody's suspicion for who I ain't. I would see some colleagues before going into those meetings who said they had my back, then I'd see them stone-faced while my world was poisoned by these vultures' droppings. And there was Mr. Winfrep, who just sat there knowing I had done well, knowing these vultures were out here to eat me, not for the good of the institution, not for the support or our students, but for their own greedy bellies hungering for power, hungered from their own emptiness.

This was the last stab, the final straw. "Let us out of here!" I could hear my characters screaming more loudly in my head every day.

Deceit is a cancer that grows in the twisted, conflicted souls of people who thrive on tearing others down. I am sure this is a human code now. I could sit there, shake their hands, and still see in their smiles, their eyes, that this was all a game and they had no other intention but directing their venom towards another's meaty leg.

Maybe I was being too sensitive, but then again, too sensitive as compared to what? I told those few friends what was going on, they saw it, but their whole thing was, "Cedric, don't worry about them. They're just trying to do this or do that. Ignore them and do what you know you have been hired to do." Okay, yeah, but, your job should not be the place where you have to dodge bullets constantly and grin at the enemy and gain points for refraining from telling your adversary to kiss your ass when he acted like a complete jerk and was being an ass. All asses should have to kiss asses together! Why don't we just take all the ignorant, aggravating asses and put them in a world together so they can worry each other to death, and God leave the rest of us alone to carry the good work on? Deep down inside me, I raged and I refused to behave as the nice, well-tamed Negro while the others were allowed to clown, frown, act down, and reap the respectable and honorable benefits they did not merit. Why was I denied that expression? I deserved to be human, too. So I would throw a rock back. I would shout their foolishness down, I would demand that they be accountable for their injury and unjust treatment of others and their irresponsible behavior. My characters' cheers filled my head.

Drift Towards Beauty, Boy

We were in the mid-nineties, which seems like ages ago. By this time I had been given a computer with email access. This allowed me to enter into whole new kinds of creating, and while at first, being old-school, I resisted, I eventually accepted it.

Soon, I became obsessed with this new tool that allowed me to work out my thoughts. Like my pen for my musical arrangements, the keys on my computer were transformative, and with them I traversed the various boundaries and distances I had from some friends, my cousin, Devonne, Mrs. Anderson, and my ideas about things. I *really* started to write, blog, image, and imagine. I could at least write my anxieties to Steve, still in LA. I shared with him my current situation. I was still a practicing, gigging musician. I had run a school, raised money, I had a great education and a Masters in a secondary, complementary field. I was young, played different music, and I had ambition. Now, being young, being ambitious, then being an outsider got me haters. The hate was a constant source of stress for me, and I was starting to lose it.

Steve encouraged me, "Bro, you have dual citizenship in that institutional world, a passport to all kinds of living zones. You are a Jew and a Roman citizen, you're like Paul." Steve was referring to the biblical Paul, of course. Wasn't he hung in the end? For these colleagues, I was just a crazy, young artist-teacher type, and they were tight at the jaw all the time. I always wondered why this was. Why couldn't these aspire, free themselves to pursue their own voices, aspirations? Of course, Rodney's call rang in my head: "Can't We All Get Along?" What would it take? These people were not much older than me, but it seems the things I tried to pursue there were ultimately a threat to some of the critical old-time players, or those who sold their short souls to the system. I was always convinced that what we did was about people, not policy and programs. Why would they rag on me for focusing on the people, the students? And why in the *hell* would they continue to focus on race? With white folks, there is a real difference between the Negroes they love to hate, love to fake, and those they just can't take. I'm in the last group, and they loved to antagonize me for it.

Institutions are run by people, so why don't the people reprogram the institution to *serve* people instead of letting themselves be gobbled up by the machine? There are always just a few of them, the vultures, but they make it real hard for you. I tried to shake them, but each day, year after year, they plotted against me, shooting down my suggestions and undermining me at every possible opportunity. I was still too much for them.

A number of us—Karen, Crystal, David, Arlington, and myself— collaborated on the idea to create a community music series, which we named after an older mentor of many of the younger teachers. This musician had been a stable member of the community for many years: Albert Tucker. He was a great teacher and community leader, and he was well-known for teaching a very successful after-school program for kids who were burdened with all kinds of high risk situations. Our group had this great idea for bringing us deeper into the community. We asked our other colleagues to consider our program, our intent to build a bridge to the community with this concert series, which would connect our students to local churches and other public school arts programs, with whom we could share auditorium spaces and increase our pool of potential new students. *A no-brainer*, I thought. The haters came up with reasons to shoot it down. At one meeting, Jack-ass started in on it: "Our resources and commitments are already stretched beyond capacity. We need to focus on increasing the quality of the program *internally*, and more importantly, increase contact time between faculty and students here at Allen to ensure we reach all our borderline students. To extend ourselves outward doesn't serve the home base need our board demanded we protect."

Well, you start suggesting anything that would upset the board and you create civil unrest among the ranks in these kinds of tight, fragile institutions. They torpedoed our outreach idea. That was alright, though, because we decided to begin the program first in the *other* institutions, bypassing the Allen system. A number of us signed off as co-coordinators. Naming the series after Mr. Tucker, in addition to what we were actually doing ignited the community, and the Mayor, old-siders from around the state, and some gray-haired donors, even a foundation, came along to boost the series. It took off, got mucho press. I didn't have to say a word because the Allen board asked Mr. Winfrep why *he* hadn't come up with such a brilliant, vibrant external outreach program. Our silence was our "we told you so." That became yet another reason the haters were more determined to foil anything I in particular came up with. Instead of looking at all this as positive growth, they turned it into their ammunition for shooting down the trouble maker.

Mr. Winfrep played it politically, not taking sides. It was difficult to know whether he liked it because it won us favor with his board members, or he hated it because he sided with his old-siders crew. Perhaps he was silently resentful that I went beyond my colleagues' hate-filled opinions and started the program anyway, or maybe he felt offended that I had gone above his head to get the endorsement of the bosses in the upper structure of the school system. Maybe he was secretly proud of me, as I had hoped, that I, his underling, had achieved something he had hoped to do. Power management is the key to understanding the human dynamics of the architecture of people in institutions.

After one of those weekly faculty meetings that heated up over something stupid, I asked Arlington Mumford, the older gentleman, something. He was Winfrep's age, his generation, which made him unpredictable, but he always said things that set my mind and my characters right. I pulled him to the side like a lost child looking for help. "Brother Arlington," I asked, "How do you maintain peace of mind?"

He said, "Little brother, let me tell you the secret: you surround yourself with things of beauty. A painting, a bonsai tree, something that allows your mind to drift past all the world's and people's ugliness. Go drift towards beauty, boy, and let it go."

I couldn't tell if this would be a passport to passivity, an acceptance of my state as a tamed, quiet, pacified Negro, or if it was a tool to sedate my growing instability.

"Little brother," he'd come at it another way. "Let me tell you something else. Wherever love shows itself, be won over by it. Take it in every time or you'll be suffocated by the evil that's always around us." Then he stepped away.

My characters warned me of their traps, even those who were my friends.

My second third-year review at Allen Academy was coming up, signaling the potential end to my four-year contract. I had passed the first one with flying colors, but tensions had been on the rise lately and I knew I'd been clashing too much with others. In the system, three consecutive good reviews and contract renewals led to tenure, making the third-year review an important factor, at least for those playing the system's game. Winfrep was silent, never letting on how he was going to advise me, steer me through, encourage me to feel confident. I could smell the corrosion of his thoughts from way down the hallway. In those weeks before the reports were due, I never saw him, but I sensed him always plotting against me. We were allowed to review our files only after he had supposedly consulted with members of the teaching team, all of whom were senior members. You don't really know who says what.

It was a very hot Friday, well into the late spring session of the school year. I was to see Winfrep at the day's end to go over the report. When it was time, I entered his office. He shut the door, said a few words of hello, put on his glasses, and began to read my evaluation like a death chart. On his desk, facing outward, was a sign which read "I have much love, but limited tolerance. Proceed with caution."

My review, from his reading, sounded horrible. Winfrep had written things that just weren't true, which he claimed were "substantiated by many colleagues who feel Mr. Sullivan disobeys the "straight line march" we hold as the very core of our principled teaching philosophy." He was completely adamant about crushing my ambition any way he could. I couldn't understand. Why? My dealings, the closeness with Mranda, were in his claw, I'm sure, but I had done well despite my entourage of haters, and I was not shy to let him know what I defined as success. I fired back immediately.

"What do you mean, "disobeys the straight line"? Because I have ideas?"

I waited for his response. He glared belligerently with scolding eyes. I went on. I knew he would say I was steering away from my students because of my ambition. "None of this takes away from me being a good listener, fair, honest, caring, and giving, that's where I want to be with my students."

He claimed I was disobedient and offered creative but "off-path resolutions to the school's preferred methods of instruction."

My classes for them were very unorthodox. I had done well with their basic music history 101 course, but I taught it *my way*. He ramped back again. "Knowing history, facts is one thing, but teaching as an academic discipline is another. You have to think about teaching music like teaching language, culture, and meaning, in context and connected. A hamburger and steak are both products of a cow. But, son, it is in seeing the ways people prepare, consume, understand a hamburger that you learn how to appreciate a steak. And then you have to eat both, of course. Cedric, you opt to put creative sauces on the meals before you bite down and taste what's already been prepared for you, man! Take a few from the old master cook here. Change your recipes, Cedric, so your meals sit well with people."

To call what I felt "disbelief" is far, far too tame—it was fucking shock mode for the suffocated souls. Of course he recognized my skills, so there were the last few sentences, which were supposed to maintain "control over the subjected" and allow a little leeway due to one's potential for success, if one obeyed: "Mr. Sullivan, while actively moving away from our methods and pedagogy, has many traits of promise, if he would chose to stay the proper course."

I sat there in that office, Winfrep glaring down on me as I read this. I couldn't believe it. All I had done and hoped I was moving towards? All those students' smiles, all that energy, all those community meetings where people were in tears due to what they saw happening in the lives of their children, all those slaps on the back and smiles from colleagues, all those board members who hugged me? And yet his sad-ass report reflected none of this in a positive way. It was as if I was off in a corner just making up my own way as I went along and barely talking to anyone else about what it all meant or how it connected. That was completely absurd!

Winfrep opened his fat mouth again. "Well, Cedric, a report is just that. It simply is a matter of detailing a few matters of direction, which are the best helpful instruction to keep you on the path of the march. This is not meant to be a letter of discouragement, just a report of potential." Yeah, but the potential of a fool it seemed. I hated this game. It did not reflect what I wanted to be on a path for, nor what we should be doing. This was more of a control mechanism for keeping people in line and under the thumb.

Yes, I fussed back at my detractors, wrote rebuffs in memos, and if stuff came up in a meeting I fought them because I believed in fighting to be me, to protect who I was. I tried to appeal to Mr. Winfrep to explain some of this, but this fell on deaf ears. I had stepped into an ideological and personality politics war in which words were thrown around loosely to gas up the rhetoric of a pseudo-community-concerns banter. If you stood against this, the group hurled suggestions of your disloyalty, effectively marking you as untrustworthy. It was divisive and distracting at best. You cannot allow these grenades to go off undetected, as it undermines the good work of many and poisons the spirit of connected work. But they kept throwing the stones and hiding the hands.

After seven years of all the games, my insides were barren, my legs and limbs torn and bleeding from all the biting dogs. My buddy Jonathan quietly told me, "Man, they're like a pack of pitbulls—once they bite into your leg, they never let go, so don't stand there long enough for them to sink in on you, keep moving and kicking that leg, swinging and circling that dog until he's dizzy and falls over." He was in a dream world. I wasn't going to waste my good energies fighting any pack of dogs. I was done.

After being a good sport for my last year, keeping the good company face and smile, filing report after report to Winfrep, I decided to resign. I was emotionally vulnerable, institutionally unprotected, and even while my initiatives had been successful, had touched everyone involved, those vultures kept at it and I had no one to watch my back. I tell you, it's not easy to be hated. It hurts. This could drive an almost-believer to get with Jesus; at least you'd have company among those who witnessed a crucifixion! We had moved away from community into this new Post-modern field of workings into a bureaucratic, personal politics machinery, the religions of success, and I couldn't bear it any more. However, I learned that persecution perfects! Persecution perfects. I was thankful for the corrections, not resentful for their attacks, really. I became stronger and wiser. They gave me tenure. I forgave them, but I didn't forget.

A part of my letter of resignation to the clan read as follows:

> *The most recent put-downs by colleagues have heightened an already-growing animosity and administrative and collegial mistrust in terms of specific ideas, duties, and ideologies in our teaching decisions that I felt were important.*
>
> *For me, the teaching community is critical. It's how I live in the world. I cannot work properly if there is not a mutual interaction, if others don't work with me to build a constructive, responsive community.*
>
> *My suggestions, good-will, and desire to achieve a working balance of all of our ideas, even if I disagreed in principle, were not appreciated. I attempted to be a good agent in my role and keep our team moving, if not on task with a project we*

were invested in, at least in consistent and good-natured dialogue. My rants to teaching colleagues, although admittedly sharp and pointed, were clearly misunderstood when they pointed at many of the things only necessary in terms of setting a fixed core of teaching policy to help better govern our decisions, particularly important for future workings for our students.

I can certainly see that my ideas are not appreciated, and my direct and passionate way of speaking and interacting does not make people feel comfortable. What makes it impossible for me to do my job is that it cannot be done in an environment of hostility toward those ideas and efforts, without others present to supplement their own ideas and efforts. It is impossible to separate myself from this environment so that I can be functional and serve at my best as a teacher at Allen Academy, because of course, my best may be fall outside the lines of our marching orders. I'm a musician: I was born to change the tempo and live sonorously.

Oh, but there was Mranda, who, through this up until the time she left, was the one who saw it all, and yet I could not touch her. She was forbidden fruit, and by law I could not dream, long for, touch, nor smell fragrances of a love that still brewed inside me. Mranda could never with me be. I had multiple pains and I was about to be ripped from all sides and down the middle all at once. I had to get out of there. I believe that when there is turmoil and pain in the streets of our community, the same energy is everywhere. I just lost hope in people caring about people and I blamed this, from my own reading and conclusions, on a larger cultural machinery. My characters whispered to me again, "Close your open door. Lock yourself in, safely inside, with people who care as you care, and who are there for you."

CEDRIC'S TRUTH: THE KIDS ON STURTEVANT STREET

That made me drift from my faith in what could be accomplished through the traditional channels. I began writing small tracks, little articles. I began passing them out, too. Just ideas, not preachy or weird, just short statements that provoked reflection. I signed those tracks, "a thought from Cedric, a friend." By that time, I had two email accounts, a new thing for me, but one was for work and one was a private one, which I printed on the track. I began to receive emails from all kinds of folks who had lost faith too. I felt comforted in this new community that seemed, although connected through invisible wires up there in the air, like it was still a connection to places we shared together. This was a space many would come to see as their home space. Some have believed, not me yet, that this would be the new place where views, values, and voices could be constructed. I worried about the corruption and deceit in that, and it being co-opted by greed. It would happen there, too.

Politics and Cultural Chaos

You still with me, friend?

After this craze within the institutions, I decided to drop the music, drop out of teaching and dealing with the anxieties of nobody listening. I was through with creating, schools, places for people to find wholeness. What about my own sanity? Where would I find peace? I know, Cedric can roll on. But I came into all this reflection during those nineties years, and I came to see how I was being pulled into my characters and how the world was crumbled up into all this. My values were under attack from the mega culturally-constructed machinery I despised, and I believed it affects what we believe, how we behave and create. These ideas we live with, we breathe them. The cultural chaos of the beginning of the 21st Century most definitely rested within greed-driven, undemocratic regimes. The signs I saw for this were clear, and I had been telling people for the last twenty years. The destruction of culture as we saw it had arrived and now all the poisoned prophets could deliver their rage-filled messages and rip against the sanctity of the soul. I saw the sequences. In 1999, the Y2K scare had everyone investing in a failed mythology: computers would shut the world down. They had been plotting against what we know, friend, was not a perfect democratic vision, but it held more promise for the common person than does the Matrix ideology these rich suits tried to construct for our society.

This time, though, I was in my routine of focusing in on all this, just contemplating what it all meant. But that Tuesday, I lost whatever sanctity and sanity my mind and characters could hold on to. I sat there and watched the world I knew surely end. Tuesday, September 11, 2001, sixty years after Pearl Harbor, a morning and mourning of unprecedented horror as those attacks brought down New York's World Trade Center, the symbol of American and global economics. It marked my consciousness. We all faced the reality of a world suddenly, it seemed, permanently changed. The sight of those planes remained with me for months; it rippled through my mind as it must have for those who lived during War World II. I needed ways to get that out of my system, my psyche.

    I decided after this I'd roam the free landscapes of my flowered mind, full of characters and ideas that always saved me from a world that (didn't) care for folks like us, you see. I was on the run again, out of Indiana. I packed my things, said my goodbyes at the end of that semester, after tenure and seven years. I was gone.

Settling in Minnesota, 2002

"Cedric, you possess everything in your powers to place yourself wherever you want to be." Oh yeah? Funny, I couldn't place myself with her.

Mranda and her words eventually melted seamlessly into the waves of selected memories, as distant as the sound of all of us playing pleasantly on Sturtevant Street, decades past. The question, the challenge of where I would "place myself" next drove me in those years more than any pre-existing plan, and I became comfortable, even obsessed, with never landing. That's my theme, you know, I don't cadence correctly. Anyway, I bought this mobile camper in those days. I figured that when all else failed, I could at least have my own wheels, complete with toilet, my own pots, a place and a pillow for my head to rest. That camper was my vehicle to the American dream, and because I could see the road ahead, at least I was determining when I was going to ride on it. And ride I did. Driving, rolling along highways became yet another way for me to find peace, an escape from places that tried to keep me locked in jurisdiction. I saw landscapes and rolling hills, trees, cows, other cars rolling in the free spaces. Those miles driving marked ways to count down to destinations that I could set and get to only if I wanted to. That became symbolically important. All through that time, I drove and drove across states in the Midwest, stopped off, parked in trailer camps, being supported only by the monies I saved from my teaching gigs, a few bar gigs as singer, and from teaching in a number of state-sponsored *ad hoc* summer arts programs.

CEDRIC'S TRUTH: THE KIDS ON STURTEVANT STREET

There was a college-owned public radio station across the territory that advertised for an internship with stipend for the development of a series of new shows. WCAM Radio, at Belmont College, News and Culture From Around the Globe and Around the Corner. Public radio, of course. I was free, why not, so I jumped at it. I drove non-stop across two states to get there. I arrived, a bit ruffled after the drive, at the receptionist's desk.

"Hi. I've driven some distance to apply for the radio intern position." A rather dry-faced, grayed, and stringy-haired woman with unmoving eyes greeted me.

"Certainly," she said, without a hesitation of procedure. She handed me an envelope and said, " Place your name on the roster there, ya?" I took it from her, trying to rip my eyes from her creepy ones. "There, ya?" I had never heard that "ya" tacked on at the end of a sentence, almost like a Canadian "eh," sounding like a question. I had arrived at another place for sure, ya?

I was still young, I felt. I had ambition and I could survive this strange land. Within a week or so after checking back they had agreed to give me an interview. Just very matter-of-fact, efficient, fair and proper, like it was the right thing for them to do. I felt surely I landed on another planet.

What I said in my interview must have impressed somebody. I was met by three nice and plainly-dressed representatives from the station: a blonde intern, Judy, a messily dressed, roughly-bearded gentleman, Marty, and an older, rather unattractive, tightly-suited woman named Amanda, who had a very warm demeanor that made this motley mix manageable. I had never done any radio before, so I was sweating.

"Well, good afternoon, Mr. Sullivan. How are you?" Amanda led the greetings and questions as the others, in evaluation mode, smiled, nodded, and sat there writing. "We've reviewed your application and letter of intent, and spoken to the director of the summer camp you listed. You have a very creative and impressive background in terms of your commitments and teaching focus. Why are you deciding to do an internship like this at this time?"

It all seemed to move in slow motion because my words became glazed with the saliva welling up in my mouth. It grabbed onto every word and weighted them down. How would I succeed in radio culture, which demands quick wit, being grounded, well-read, and rounded? I swallowed hard and I began. "Well, I love radio, always have. I have become a bit worn by the daily grind of teaching administration, although I loved my teaching. I really want to write and focus my energy in other areas now. I have always been a fan of public radio and believed I could be a host, actually."

"Really, why?" She inquisitively pushed and perked up slightly more. I got a rise, and so I rode it.

"I like sending ideas that matter into the air. And I've thought a lot about how messages are received. In the classroom, on the stage, reaching people is what I have always done. But radio is a very special kind of transmission because it is personality-driven. I like that touch. Growing up, I always practiced having a radio voice. Didn't care about being seen."

They all kind of got more comfortable, less tight, as if I had stumbled into one of the zones they could better relate to. Radio people are interesting. Marty with the beard spoke up.

"You may not know this, but radio is not a profitable business. We have to provide a service to thousands of listeners, but most of us are, like you mention, interested in broadcasting for some of the same reasons. It's a powerful way to reach people. So we have to depend on the college endowments and advertising. Internships are a way for us to creatively draw talent that many times eventually become our core. And, we *have* had, um, more seasoned interns like yourself." That stuck with me.

There were more exchanges as the others chimed in and forgot their Minnesota frost-freeze for the moment. After a while the blonde, Judy, began.

"Clearly, you have the interests; your writing and administrative experience help here. But what else do you think you can share with us that would help us achieve some of the goals of our new development, which is really the heart of the new programming initiative?"

"I'm excited mainly in new program development, creatively engaging new areas." They all perked up a bit more. My words were flowing more freely now, and I was feeling more confident. "Radio can deliver, delight, and create a place where an audience can come freely, over and over again. Why not work to create spaces that allow people to be so moved? New programs should be put in place to draw newer sponsors, new audiences looking for a different space to be in. If the people continue to come to that unique space we could create, surely your advertisers and sponsors will want to meet them there." I had figured out by this time that conscientious, good-willed free thinking doesn't pay. It was the keyword "advertisers" that got them. People in business want to focus on the bottom line. I sold them a line and they took it.

I was in. I thought of Patrick and imagined he'd be proud of me. I ended up moving into a place up in Northern Minnesota.

I was focused again. I surveyed the place, saw people who were focused I could connect to, and we all buried ourselves in the work of creating a better broadcast station with innovative programs that would draw the audience and the new sponsors.

The work, initially, was easy. I made the transfer. In radio, it's not the ideas, it's the delivery. Writing ideas was not the problem; what I had to learn was how to frame the ideas in a palatable way, not written down, not "teached or preached," but that echoed across the airwaves. I spent a year or so perfecting the delivery. During the busywork of writing short ad copy, researching stories, editing news shows, and working the phones for the funding campaigns, I was working on my radio voice, waiting for a chance to create my own show.

I was able to edit a few national public radio shows, some local news and culture pieces, and soon I had developed enough chops that they invited me to create a new feature story show. I was most interested in a way to provide commentary on contemporary culture. The world of classical music in public radio certainly had its place, but as a contemporary artist I believe we were faced with the daunting task of making the stuff relevant to our audience's everyday lives. I convinced them that it was equally important to break down the categorical boundaries in our culture that separate people, such as music. I tied Beethoven's rhythms to Prince's rhythms and Bob Dylan's songwriting to Franz Schubert, Ellington's orchestrations to Ravel's. We took a look at the relevance of hip hop, can you believe it? We pressed the box to the cliff and pushed it over for a classical music station. I convinced them that there was a listening audience out there who looked for the broader, more diverse, hip and intelligent, moving music and culture programming. The Urban Music Café became my dream project, which I imagined could be a weekly topical commentary feature on music and culture. Radio, the last free-ideas zone. Better than tracks, classes, and I had gotten tired of being trapped in the MacBook and Internet box. I grew up and away from my infatuation with Neo, the electronic mail and pretty lights generation.

The Urban Music Café was a multi-platform radio show that mixed an urban jazz-art-classical-world-hop playlist with commentary and culture discussion from prominent guests through interviews, poetry, and studio music performances that were patched in from other public music stations around the country. One of the ads was: *Cedric's Music Café is a place you stop by to listen to the best and varied music and art perspectives, hear about what music, life, and living mean, and how it all connects to modern daily life.*

I was the host with the vibe. We created theme music and publicity tags like *Urban Music Café: music, culture, and talk for the connected and concerned; Music that hip didn't hop over, but landed in your pocket.* Our audiences felt the ambiance, we created a sound-mind space that listeners could feel and hear, as if they were walking into an imagined café with music, great tasting food, good people, and a show with special guest stars who had something to say.

Even though the Urban Music Café was really located and broadcast from rural Minnesota, it was a cosmopolitan café "you know, in your own city." We prided ourselves in saying "all you need to do is stop in, sit down, chill out, and have a listening meal, a couple of sound bites, something really delicious and satisfying." The beautiful, magical thing about music on the radio is that it's portable; you can take it with you anywhere, and it transports you to places from within the air. During my second year there, I had a poet who frequently visited the show whose name was J. Otis Pommer, and he loved music, all kinds. J. Otis was a big guy who walked liked a ballet dancer. It was uncanny. He'd come in dressed loud as hell with a big hat, jingling boots, and, no matter what season, colorful wool shawls wrapped around him that announced his coming before you discerned his bright, dark brown face. His voice was intriguing and gracious, strong with conviction, and tender, like a child telling you of his toys and dreams. When you heard him read, you were swept into this idea-world that only he had the keys to, then he locked you in there. I loved what he taught us about imagery, line, and using your mind to live. I played the music that ran along his stories and danced with his characters, and provided the sonic punch lines to his vivid poems, compelling questions, and flowered worlds.

His first appearance on the show sealed the appreciation and validation for what we were doing among my colleagues there.

He mused, "Music that I can truly hear and feel is the result of one thousand cuts into the soul of people by domination and abuse. That music screams of injustice, hatred, eco-political and social disenfranchisement, and if those people could bleed into a cup, it would taste and sound like the Blues."

Calls were streaming in. People loved the edge we brought to the regular white lines of stories about pretty and bored housewives in St. Paul lamenting shopping at the Mall of America. I had live performances, where my guests played music and tried to project this place where you could always tune in and get this good stuff. I always opened my show with "Let me say it to you this way: at the end of the day, what means and has its way is how the music matters and stays, so let the music play."

Our program director, Marty, also assumed some of the fundraising, directed, produced, and edited my scripts. Our engineer was the dedicated Lianne Horn. She pulled our show in, made it sound produced and polished. Lianne could edit together a scratchy voice with a sound effect, add wind in the background, link my botched sentences, and by the time you heard it all put together, you'd think our programs were on location all over the planet with a full team of reporters. Man, we were a team.

Marty would say to me with such love in his voice, as if radio was his precious child, "Cedric, with radio, it's all about creating a voice that connects to people with a warm familiarity. Radio is about direct connection. People really value their time with their *personality*, their radio person. They believe in who you say you are. Practice your radio voice, Cedric, practice that voice so people come to know the personality of your sound." In radio you have to learn to make even the bad sound good. I worked on my speaking voice over and over until I could melodically and lyrically pronounce a horrific sentence, curse, or say nonsense. Funny, I would go places and it wasn't my face people knew: they knew the sound, my voice.

Of course, my characters loved this because they got to be fluid and practiced too. The idea of finding voice stayed with me. I would drive out to the small college station once a week, with three or four shows typed up, my CD's and tapes, and we'd go to laying in shows. The audience response was tremendous. I didn't have a gig. I didn't have a record contract. I didn't have a paid job, really, but I had a voice. That voice reached people. I had plenty of topics to deal with. Our listenership had grown and there was talk of expanding the show nationwide. I could write a solid salary for a few years, with staff, writers. This would work. Marty and I began to get busy writing the grant proposals. My weekly work was supported with a small stipend, which covered my meals and the rent for my small apartment. I lived without frills, and spent the days unashamed of my spartan living because, unlike Los Angeles, and the wear and tear of living in downtown Indianapolis, Minnesota just ain't stressing you.

On weekends, I'd drive down to Minneapolis and St.Paul. I walked the huge lakes, canoed Lake Calhoun, attended all the free street festivals. There were state-supported museums, there were theaters and free live music, poetry slams. I could live there, develop my radio shows, and just be on the air creating this comfortable airspace. I loved, *loved* it!

One day, I received a memo, an email.

CEDRIC'S TRUTH: THE KIDS ON STURTEVANT STREET

From: Marty
To: Cedric

Cedric. I'm very sorry to inform you that we need to cut the Music Café Show. The board wants to move to a more "news and culture" centered format, and they don't think your show flows with their new direction. This will go into effect in four weeks. I am really sorry Cedric.

All of a sudden, my whole world was flipped. The world was suddenly into this sensationalist-media hype, and I'd been reduced to a sound bite to be deleted. It's just all about somebody else's idea about the money chase, really. *There must be a theme looming here, always bringing me dissonant chords.* Good God Baraka help me! I had become the Blues people. The plain faced Minnesotans were emotionless. Lake Woebegone had frozen over! No one bothered to appeal to the listeners for their take. No one talked to me. No one suggested creative changes to fuse the new interests or needs. They just cut, cut out the show and cut open my throat, cutting off my voice, stabbing me in the back and twisting the blade into my ideas.

I became disillusioned with their new program tactics. The funding I was promised never came through, and I had to close up shop. To make matters worse, the entire small station was bought out by a huge corporate owner, Clip-Channel Industries, a larger radio giant that played smooth jazz and sold shit, once again! I got cut and thrown out just as I had been with the record company in LA, Michelle's school, Claude's, and Allen Academy! That was a lot of stuff, too many kicks, and twenty years had gone by and, wow, I was really going batshit insane!

Devonne Divine Digs

What did I do then? You know what, friend? I had to live in some other worlds for a good while to keep me sane.

I relaxed into the world of films: *Logan's Run, Blade Runner, Terminator,* and my favorite, *The Matrix.*

In my favorite scene from *The Matrix,* Morpheus asks Neo: "Do you believe in fate, Neo?

"No."

"Why not?"

"Because I don't like the idea that I'm not in control of my life."

"I know *exactly* what you mean. Let me tell you why you're here. You're here because you know something. What you know you can't explain, but you feel it. You've felt it your entire life, that there's something wrong with the world. You don't know what it is, but it's there, like a splinter in your mind, driving you mad. It is this feeling that has brought you to me… You can feel it when you go to work… when you go to church… when you pay your taxes. It is the world that has been pulled over your eyes to blind you from the truth."

"What truth?"

"That you are a slave, Neo. Like everyone else you were born into bondage. Into a prison that you cannot taste or see or touch. A prison for your mind."

Morpheus offers two pills, and Neo takes the pill for truth.

For me, truth is a journey toward discovery. I see past the recent days characterized by lies, greed, hypocrisy, and corporate political tyranny and terror that have claimed and attempted to shape the contorted identity of our day. For all of us, this is a chance to rethink the commitments to what it could mean to continue toward "Cedric's campaign for the cultural causes." This reflection will not completely right the wrongness of our complex history and society, but push us to make a conscious effort to be a part of the solution, of future improvement. My characters push me.

From whatever side you view it, we all are trying to replicate or maintain worlds of being, to create or dissuade or seek truth. I love baking oatmeal cookies now, just like the Matrix Oracle. After she gave you wisdom, she'd give you a cookie to munch on while you contemplated the truth you'd eventually reach. I'd started mixing my dough with walnuts, cranberries, hazelnuts, and pinches of cinnamon and orange peels, expecting my friends, or anyone who would eat them, to discover what was in it as we talked.

The trailer I bought allowed me a home on the road, a kitchen on wheels, my own personal 24-hour movie theater, a portable studio, an office ready to go, and sanity. I escaped into a self-sufficient world that left me and my characters too busy to be bothered by anyone. I began to see myself as a runner, traversing the worlds between the trap, the Matrix, and the pursuit of truths. We are truth-seekers. I called my cousin Devonne once to check in. She, like you, probably thinks I'm a bit off, too.

"Cuz, this is off! Damn straight. Is nothing easy, is it always so complicated? Ced, you think too much. You give me a brain cramp!"

I shot back, "But I like the movies, they help me work through my questions. I see them in there."

"Ok. That's cool, but why can't you like them because they are entertaining? Why so philosophical and off the deep end for you?"

"Because they have meaning, Devonne. People are searching for meaning all the time, through all kinds of places. It's not just about entertainment, the whole world spins this out. The whole world has taken creativity and turned it into entertainment. That's what I'm dealing with all the time. They have taken our messages and our life, our meanings, and turned our stories into entertainment." For the first time in years, I thought I could make her see.

"So, Cedric, you want to be a purist when it comes to creativity, is that what you're saying? You don't what your creativity to end up in the hands of a conglomerate for entertainment purposes? Is that it, Cuz?"

"Damn right. Well, that's my job as an artist. To make sure I stay on the path of truth, to make sure people don't take that truth and turn it into something else for a sale."

"Wait, wait, Cuz, hold on! So tell me again, why do you like these movies again? They are entertainment-based, right, and *you*, like them?"

"But I like them, because they move beyond the entertainment, allow glimpses for people to examine what the real battles are. That's what you don't understand, Devonne. That's what I have been about. Some of us have to be on the front lines of the real battles, the battle for your soul. I'm a truth seeker. That's what I've been teaching these kids, how to find their truths."

She wasn't seeing it. "Cuz, what's your truth?"

"My truth is to find *me*! And if your truth is to find you, then we have this journey together that allows us to find our true humanity, which the man is trying to keep us away from, the man and his machines!"

"Here we go again, Cedric. The "man" conspiracy theory again I'm sick of hearing all this. I love you, Cuz, but I don't understand you. I think you have smoked too many gym shoes or something!"

"Well, it's all the same game—and how do you smoke a gym shoe, anyway, Devonne? That's ridiculous."

"I don't know, but since you seeking truth and all, you'll find a way to smoke a gym shoe!"

"That's just the problem. Nobody is willing to take the risk, to stretch, to try to understand the other. If you don't understand me, how can we move together so I understand my truth when I find it? If anyone is to understand me, it should be you. You are all I've got left." I thought after saying that, she might get it.

"Ced, you have been given so much—your life is a beach, kid!"

"Oh, really, Devonne, you really think so? Nobody ever gave me anything. I never won any contests. Yes, I was given opportunities, people, against the odds, took chances on me. And I made the most of those opportunities: I made in-roads and connections. I've had to dig sometimes, though, and I've fallen in holes and had to crawl out and start again from scratch."

"Cuz, I really don't get you most times. Beneath our skin, threaded around our bones, we all have a complex web of conditions and circumstances. You have to work those out, Ced."

I could hear the voices inside me raging. "What does she know about us?" Some other voice inside yelled back, "Nothing! Leave the accusers to think of us the way they want. We stand as I stand!"

"Cuz," Devonne reasoned again. "You are going to have to face your own demons and monsters to be able to sleep with yourself in the dark rooms of your everyday. Cuz, I understand, you want to find your truth out there in Minnesota, but—"

"Devonne, I'm not trying to say it's one-way, either, or done in a day. It's a whole journey toward clarity. I'm trying to move towards finding it, then defining it. I send it out everyday, and music is my ambassador."

"I'm just trying to say that when you find it, Cuz, don't deny your truth!"

"On my radio show, I felt like I was moving closer and closer to it, and then it didn't work out… I *need* to find my truth, my sanity!"

"Ok, I'm gonna try to pull you back from the edge, Cuz. We've gone over this before. You're spinning, Cuz. Spinnin', spinnin' here. Even though you don't call enough for me to help you work through this more often— but that's another story. You think everybody is out to get you, don't you? Ced, you only die after you've stopped living, so it's far better to bury your pains in the joys of living. It's plain survival, Ced."

"Devonne, doesn't everything I've told you add up to the fact that they all are trying to keep me from obtaining the truth?."

"Ok, Cuz, not really. Cuz, I think people are not ready for your truth. I think you already know your truth. You keep searching for it, but people don't understand your truth. Every time you get an opportunity to tell your truth, seems like your mouth gets taped up. So, Cedric, look at it this way. Who cares if they don't understand you? Who cares, Cuz, what does that matter? You're being true to yourself. I wish I could tell you. I tried to tell you this before you left California. I'm mad 'cause I don't even have an address to send you a Christmas card! I got caller ID, but what good is that when all it tells me is you're calling from a pay phone? That's wrong, Cuz, but that's *your truth*. So operate in it! Grab a hold of yourself, focus, bro. I've got to go, Ced. I've got to go and find some truth and get me something to eat. I love you. Bye!"

She hung up and that was it, the last I heard from her. She was a bit upset. I knew she loved me, but she didn't understand. I was done with trying to help her to truth, and I was tired of trying to make the others see, too.

Songs For Saving Souls

"Cedric, my man, be sure to get the to the ocean, some water, where the seagulls and the breezes fly free... That's the best for inspiring the creative idea."

My old friends from the Leimart Park area used to tell me this all the time. Now, years later, I was a long way into the middle of America's hungry belly, living isolated in the Midwest. No oceans in Minnesota. I did, however, find this place where I could search for my soul again—perhaps even find it. I found some peace in Stillwater, a small town on the St. Croix River, thirty miles or so east of the Twin Cities. The spot seized my senses, caught my inspiration by its tail and flung me widely about in its poetic spins. I landed on my feet again every day, relieved. I loved this spot because it challenged me to chase away my demons and destroy my cages, unlock them—this place made me feel like a child again, someone who could roam freely and discover the world. As an adult you have to constantly rebuild your internal homes, refinance your mental and mortal mortgages, but this place afforded me a much-needed break. I sat there day after day, on a bench overlooking the water. Week upon week in that summer I forced myself to introduce me to me again. I'd drive back to the Twin Cities filled with thoughts of beginning again somewhere else, just disconnecting from this network.

There was this pastry shop there, and no ordinary one. They made an apple cinnamon fritter dripping in butter that no one could even begin to understand, no matter how many times or how hard I tried to explain it. It's those kinds of places, things, that stick with you. You remember fondly. You had to get there by 8:30 am to get one dripping, piping hot fritter. People always bought three or four a visit. They ran out quick. Besides the peace of mind, there was that run for the dough that helped secure this place as part of my entry back to myself. That aroma of hot, buttery dough that could only be helped down with hot creamy coffee was as sweet and sensible as any melody Mozart or Elton could create. When I got off the freeway, crossed the waters of the St. Croix, went over the bridge and through the tunnel covered with greens vines that pointed me to Nancy's Mother Memories, my whole body and psyche confirmed that I had arrived. Do you know those kinds of places? They just sit *right* in your soul as if it were made perfect just for you. You have to have the spots that you hang in. The older I get, the more desperately I search for those kinds of spots; they matter, they make you right.

Sitting there day after day, dreaming into the light ripples of that water, slowly swallowing my pastries, sipping my coffee, I really started to think about meaning outside any institution, band, or talk about what it did or I did. I decided after countless gigs, teaching, and radio shows that nobody really *listened* to me.

I would write a book, *Songs For Saving Souls*, and write my narrative, my story. *What if music was salvific? What would we have in our hands then?* I thought. I dropped out of sight and the months and years that lagged are blurred. Renewal and sustenance of our sanity and the sanctity of our souls sometimes comes at great costs, but I wrote that book and it will speak for me.

I had kept in touch with a few friends. Stephen I emailed when I could. Mrs. Anderson got a letter or two, and Devonne I called by pay phone, so she knew things.

I was on the road in my trailer reading and writing everything voraciously, imaging a world my characters could live in.

There's this street there in St. Paul, Summit Avenue. It must be one of the most beautiful streets I have ever driven along. Maybe it's just because it reminded me of Chicago Boulevard or Outer Drive, similar streets that wound around the entire city of Detroit. There were maple trees that reached out and cast cool shadows over the entire concrete trail in the summer. Those lawns were just like the ones I remembered from Sturtevant Street, but bigger, grander, sprawling around and around, back and up the side of the homes, so neat and well-taken care of. The street *smells* of prestige, a good, hard-earned, unpretentious prestige. It's a Midwest thing. As a child we marveled at similar homes in Detroit along streets like these: they seemed occupied by people who had arrived and had it all together. On this long Summit Avenue wind are the houses, huge and classic Victorians that line up next to one another for miles, from the banks of the Mississippi, then melting into the cosmopolitan downtown area. One day, I kept driving along Summit Avenue, through downtown, until that winding road led me to the parking lot of a rather obscure-looking building. The sign outside read "Last Stop Faith Ministries." I stopped, parked, and went inside. I don't know why. I was just tired of rolling for the moment. You asked, that's where I'd been. These past few years, I'd been teaching again in St. Paul without anyone knowing it; I'd been leading a choir, actually, in an unlikely institution for this "sinner."

I thought, *Maybe they'll find me soon.*

The church embraced me after a few months, and as I shared with them what I did, they invited me to work with their young people. I decided to participate in this babysitting and train the youth choir while I figured it all out again. You got me, friend? I had to take my last stance.

I get the church thing and what the preacher does. He saves souls once. Ah, but the musician saves somebody's soul every night and again and again.

There was that awful college visit I made, remember? I held the students up in an auditorium with a plastic gun pointed at my head. Can you believe that? I know, really stupid. So in the swirl of that craziness, I decided to find peace in preparation where no one would find me. I decided I should go underground, with a new name and a lasting purpose, and where better than Minnesota? That's why I was back in St. Paul, but driving aimlessly took me exactly where I wanted to be—I ended up joining that church!

You know, I have never been religious at all. I'm not trying to be no preacher these days, either, but we need to be encouraged, to be faithful to any inspiration that fosters a belief towards some journey to truth. Clarity in life is salvific. Since that day I ended up in that parking lot and walked in, I will never forget nor again be so marked as I was by the ministry of the pastor there. They call him the righteous Reverend Dr. Ray Himmings. The message that day resonated so, so deeply inside of me, with all the things I wanted to be about in the world in that moment. I'm glad I landed there.

"You see, cracking a boulder with one hundred blows of a sledge hammer doesn't rattle or move it. But now, it is the one hundred and first blow that does it. You couldn't see the mounting, and the connecting of all the smaller cracks that converged beneath the hardened surface. It was those underlying connections you were making that caused the boulder to crack." He poured on more wisdom and wit in his delivery than you could buy in a bookstore. "Vision is caring, consecration, and commitment," he announced freely. I was totally moved toward getting to that kind of truth again. In a church? Well, truth sits where it is needed the most, I guess.

I can't get it out of my mind or off of my soul. The sermon said to answer your calling again. The reverend kept emphasizing that you must find your creative source and be committed to that. What is your commitment, your calling, and are you willing to do the work of that calling? He kept saying, "We must answer humbly, and act boldly." He encouraged the congregation to center not on just any career, but on their callings. He pointed out that the word career stems from the French word for racetrack. I didn't know this. He took his scripture, I think, from John 21: 15-19. That bible verse I did remember: "Do you love me more than these? Then feed my sheep. Feed my sheep, follow me and feed my sheep. Cast your nets where you are, to the right and you shall find." I think that's how it goes, and in the story the hearers and followers were not able to pull up the net because it was filled with more fish than they believed they could find. That did it for me. I was hooked.

So back to your question: why here? Like I said, I joined this church because I landed there. I connected to folks and they had an active young people's ministry in the city, and I had to give, share. I just felt that if any place had that ritual, communal thing and connected to music and meaning, it would be the church, especially the Black church. I wasn't completely a heathen, you know. "Mom's and them" brought a brother up right. With all the attack, with all the shortcomings of it, after all the pomp and circumstance, the Black church is still the most important cultural institution Black folks have today, and it's been that way since slavery days. You know, when you look at the culture, there are all kinds of connections that are made. Politics, music, preachers, literature, dance, artwork, poetry, social philosophy, dance, some meals, and church. They make a lot of fun of the Black church in movies these days. I remember the scene with James Brown being the preacher of the church, in that Blues Brothers movie, and him dancing and hooping it up and all with the choir—that's real. That should tell you something. You have to have a preacher who gets it, though, really gets it. All those things have to come together: the spirit and the word, the truth, the music, the community. In my adult life, I was never much of a church-going person. I changed my tune this time.

Of course I remember all that Black church ritual thing from my youth, the call and response, the deacon and deaconesses in their white uniforms. All the pre-church testimonies with all the deacons using the slave church, lining out, "Ahhh, ah, ahhh, I Love the Lord, he heard, he heard, he heard, my, myyyy cry." This used to get me because this was the one place that people did remember the slave traditions of the old getting-down community thing. Then those sisters would get up, "Giving honor to God, who is the head of my life. Brothers and sisters, I have a testimony this morning." "Yes Sir, ya do, yes ya do, now say it now," a very righteous deacon yelled out in agreement.

And of course right before the Reverend speaks there's the hymn of preparation that the choirs sing, because, like I told you, the churches I came up in around Detroit had the choirs that could set it all up, then raise the dead. Magnificent choirs, voices, such pageantry, so powerful. I don't think white folks lay it out so beautifully like this. When that choir stood up, you knew folks were going to sing, baby *sing*! The director motioned the musicians, drummer, bass, piano, and organ and with one finger, motioned for the choir to sway, in beat, left, right, and awwwww, it got going.

"Come and go with me, to my father's house. I said, come and go with me" The melodious spoken-word, half sung, half-preached thing they do was big with us, and it connected. Sometimes the preacher would pray down on his knees, on the preachers bench. And when he rose to speak we had been properly prepared to hear something that was always, always the main moment.

This preacher at Last Stop spoke about things that were not just religious—they were relevant, and he spoke with such skill and vitality, with spiritual meaning that his words easily cut across the generation lines in that congregation.

"…As people living in this time, the post prophetic period, I am sure that what we are missing is a people perspective, spirit, mindset of dignity, a common belief system, some depth in our hope, sense of purpose, a plan of action among communities, a value of humanity, civility, a stride for excellence, an understanding among and of ourselves, and perhaps it needn't be written, but worn outwardly like a fashion statement. To ensure we still remember these, guiding aesthetics, or a sound, poetry, some signs that slice across our social divides and affirm our oneness."

He stepped down off the podium, and with his demeanor rejected what seemed reserved for only the noble souls in the world. He was with us, on the floor, shaking hands as he moved forward, as if to say "I'm down here with you sister, brother." He went on.

"What happened to that fight for our survival, for greatness? I don't hear it, see it, feel it, sense it. I don't see this embraced at the macro-cultural level. I know too, there are workers in the fields, community heroes, artists, churches, programs across the urban horizons which we don't celebrate because we simply don't get to hear about them. I live for what remnants of hope are left, for the beauty in life, for those who try to grasp those remnants. I miss the gleam, the excitement, the innocence that is to be in the eyes of a curious and perplexed young student who simply wants to know, because the pursuit of knowing is a value that arms one's accomplishments and shapes the life."

"Uh-huuuh, I know you can't hear this, I know you feel kind of uncomfortable, but God keeps a pillow and a cushion to comfort your bare side. You don't need nothing fancy with God. Uh-huuh."

I was there with him on this like never before, and in this place I sensed a connection I hadn't found until then.

"How, how, how you, how me, how her, mister? How we? We have to collectively sing, re-script the values, dream, create, work, build, and be together in multiple forms, in all kinds of ways in different places, all the time. So I end, but we send our calls to order, a call to the chosen flock." The organist then cued the drummer, guitar player, bass, and choir to did two hits on a chord every time the pastor said "Uh-huh, yessir." Just like James Brown would instruct. "Uh-huh, yessir."

Then the church band did two music hits. Chord, chord. "And I am made most sure that the God I serve has made you a promise today, uh-huh, yessir, to meet you where you live, flavor your thinking with a message for our times that is seasoned with the good flavor, uh-huh, yessir, and it will be imprinted deep within your souls, born and worn in your spirit and everyday evident in the way you walk, talk, that no man can mock, yessir..."

The parishioners were on their feet, clapping, amen-ing, and the choir was setting in on the call to discipleship. By the time he finished, folks would be lining up in the isles to join the church, be a part of this ministry, this message with meaning. And you know the music was right there with it all, threading it all together. That made me move in different directions. I was sold again, right there.

Now it doesn't matter where, how, why. I had found a moment to share and for then, I was there. I told the pastor my name was Sullivan Cedrics, that I had been a teacher and had worked with the young people's choirs. I hoped he didn't listen to public radio. It was my voice out there, not my face. I was seen there as contributing to the community and even gave a few talks. In that church, I really started preaching to everybody. They started calling me Brother Cedrics.

I didn't find the voices nor the young people at Last Stop particularly inspiring, but rather needy, just missing stuff. They were there, though. They were there and in numbers, for some strange reason. I thought, *There must be some creative kids in all this here for me to connect with.* I was sure of it, even in a sleepy church youth choir, and besides, songs *are* for saving souls.

Your Cutting Edge

"You sit down right there, and stay put till your father finishes, Junior. Read one of these magazines and snack on your caramel corn. I'll be back before you both are finished. Stop crying and be a big boy. You in here with men folks now!"

The young mother admonished her disgruntled youngster, pointing at a chair, before sitting him down amongst the men and then leaving to tend to other things.

Besides the church, I really connected to the local barber shop, Your Cutting Edge. It was the cultural center, the neighborhood barber shop. For Black folks in St. Paul, this was *the* place to go for a cut. Everybody was always up in there, from the preacher to the dealer: politicians, teachers, businessmen, professors, "playas," and college students. And The Edge, as we nicknamed it, had some real living characters in it. I could let my hair down and just hang out with these guys. In the whole city, these were the people I talked to most, where I connected to the people again, even though I worked in the church. That really wasn't going to heal my wounds of late.

Much like James Weldon's Black Society in his *Ex-Colored Man*, here, too, you could see glimpses of our whole Black world. We were all in there, at the Edge. The guys there had all kinds of wisdom, bringing a noise, junk, mess, fun, and soothing karma that grounded me, bringing me back to reality. There was Cool-Nute, the peacemaker, my barber; Snowman, the older wise dude who took no shit off nobody; Nellwood, from Haiti, the owner of the shop; and

Winston from the islands, they both brought their global perspective to the table, knowing which roti and rice and curry shops were the best, what music was in. There was Big Keith, the most well-read and the most opinionated guy there, who fought with everybody on every issue, and who, while generating the most anger, got the biggest respect; the other barbers, Shawaun, Damon, and Poncho, quietly and cautiously listened as the lead speakers and info-seekers led all the discussions in the shop with all the customers. And while they were a bunch in themselves, the clientele at the Edge were even more fascinating to watch and listen to.

One day, a customer walked in. The client, a regular, was a rather stately-looking gent dressed in a striped tan sports jacket, unbuttoned dress shirt, slacks, and shined shoes, and he carried a dull, worn leather satchel. Keith immediately started in on him.

"So look who's walking up in here today, in the man's crossover suit. I thought you were down with the people, bro, you done sold us out too, huh?"

"I know this Negro didn't just say some crazy shit, right?" He spoke in the most unruffled and proper voice, deep and smooth. The entire shop ripped into laughter. Somebody shouted out. "You know nobody in here pays Big Keith no mind."

The radio was the friendly noise that sung everybody's name, cemented the groove, and reported on the latest sports scores and news events. That sense of community, of familiarity was what I missed about life, like those days on Sturtevant Street, where everybody knew your name, and even if you decided to change it for the day, it was ok 'cause everybody could tell you how to respell it a dozen different ways. They all walked with you through your maze.

The traffic noise outside on Selby Drive provided the only proof that there was actually another world somewhere, because once you entered the Edge, you stepped into a world unto itself. Posters of Muhammad Ali, Tupac, and Maya Angelou were proudly hung on the walls, our icons of culture. Magazine racks display the Wall Street Journal, Ebony, and Newsweek, and of course the hairstyle magazines that held every possible haircut you could ever want. The shop always served caramel corn and coffee, too, which you could smell from a block away.

The respectable gent continued. "No, no, Keith, I quit today, as a matter of fact. I don't owe the man downtown nothing. I'm starting my own business, going my way, like Nellwood here did it."

Snowman started in, "I *told* you I saw Jeanine and her two babies round the way, and she said brother man here was going into his own business. That's how you do it the right way, for yourself. That's what I been telling these tired-assed brothers around here for a while. Do your thang, and watch 'em line up to come your way. That's what I'm talking 'bout." Snowman was always dressed in the traditional white cloth barber's jacket, sported an equally white beard, and possessed a slow cautious walk and a very particular way of looking deeply into you, peering over the rims of his cracked glasses. He moved to the back of the narrow shop to read his waiting crumpled newspaper.

There were always the exchanges, the music, sports and news reports blaring as the backdrop of the never-ending stream of discussion, which ranged from baseball scores, to which of these rappers was making the most money, to the presidential debates, to why old-school music was better, to Oprah Winfrey, to recipes. It was the most happening joint in all of St. Paul. I loved my time in that barber shop, and I could see myself being found there. They knew me as the music man round the church way.

The recently entered customer hung up his jacket and continued with Big Keith. "Well, I saved my cash, sent my old lady away to be with her family for a few down South, and I am, as the Snowman says, taking some time for myself to work it all out. I seen this coming from a long ways back. I was always interested in real estate. I have a way with people, and I know good deals. I do my homework, and I like the idea of helping people find a good place to live. All kind of places to help people move to. I've been studying the trade for a long while, now I'm ready to get my license, and do this. You see my brothers, when you reach fifty and beyond in life you know more things.

"At twenty, thirty, you have just been lifted out of the womb, somebody slaps you on the ass, and you are crying, opening your eyes. You don't know what you think you might like to know, when you figure out it's the right time to start asking. But at fifty, with some wisdom, you know to ask for the right steak, cooked at just the right temperature, for the just perfect glass of right wine, and with the combination of good company and conversation, with friends who will relieve you of the stress you will inevitably encounter when dealing with the twenty dumb-asses you will have to deal with in the coming week."

The entire shop bursts into howls.

A young man rushes in, a regular. "Yo, dawg, I told you, mad-dawg stupid shine plus with the Mcquiers, Mack, playa!!"

Winston interrupted. "How many times I told you, young son, nobody bark in here. We are full-grown men, not dogs!"

Cool-Nute interceded, "Ah, he's cool, lay off the young blood, he's just trying to lay on you a few goods." Winston chidingly rang back. "That's not my point, Nute. I like his product, but I don't like his sales methods in here."

The young man continued. "Winston the island-wind jammer, I mean no harm. Your customers like my products, and I like to let 'em know what's happening with the goods. I'm just properly representing." The men shouted back their agreement, and a few pulled him over to their chairs, while waiting for their cuts, to peer through his bags of CD's for the week's good deals.

"Cool-Nute, man, what's going on with your brother and his lady, man? Dummy to let her go!" Nellwood, a deeply-committed family man himself, was always ready to give the advice in the shop.

"My brother and his love triangles—hey, what can I tell you? What's the song you old dudes swoon to, "Me and Mrs. Jones, we got a thing going on," you know the one?" Ears had perked up and everybody was howling. Those days at the edge were always full of people with dreams, some with busted lives, some who could tell you everything about living rightly. These were proud, successful, wonderful men, and some were clowns who talked foolishness, too. That's what made the Edge percolate, and I was always plugged in, for the moment. Any day in the Edge you could hear the charged exchanges. On a Monday evening, a Saturday morning, days leading up to or after an election. There was always someone and something for the guys to get into. It was a *righteous* place.

"Fellas, fellas," another local reverend, James Carrington Casey was in the Edge for his weekly Tuesday evening cut. He was always dressed in a black suit with a preacher's collar, holding a handkerchief in one hand and his cane in other. He was the kind of preacher everybody liked. He was no cartooned community character, and he was studied, but he hung with the people. He could talk with and be among the folks.

"I'm speaking at my church this Sunday on Men's Day. You have no excuse. I'm just telling you now. You men folks 'round here don't go to church anymore."

A few good-spirited fellows joined in, "What you talking 'bout, Reverend? I go to church!" "Me too!" "Me three!" A few more chimed in. He continued. "And to get it, you have to come early in the morning when the good getting is good. Eight in the morning!"

"What you dealing with, Pastor?" Nellwood created the calm.

"I'm speaking on men's friendships. How we have to cultivate a strong, supportive, special bonding that the world needs today."

"On this Sunday, huh?" Another gentleman asked, never lifting his head from his newspaper. Another guy piped up, "I was hoping you'd say Wednesday night, Reverend. At least I could pass through after I hit a few balls at the golf course way out near you."

"No, Sunday, I said Sunday morning. Yep, Sunday, just like you being here. You come to the barber shop, you can come to church, same thing."

"Eight o'clock? How do you expect me to get up that early?" Cool-Nute was known as the party-playa, always hanging. He had a good eye for that.

"What do you mean man? You get up to go to work don't you? You can get up to go to church. Don't go out this Saturday night, you'll be just fine, Cool-Nute."

The Edge rolled in laughter, everybody knew the deal.

"Reverend brother, I likes you and all, but only love makes a man leave bed and get up early for church. I ain't a married man, so I don't got no good reason to get up for *nobody* on no early Sunday morning." One of the younger men shared. Reverend Casey was never one to let up, so he came right back at him. "Yeah, I bet if Beyoncé or Rihanna was there, you'd get up to see that, right"?

"Yeah but I can listen to Beyoncé on the radio for free, after I wake up."

There was good-hearted laughter all around. "Well, young man, I'll just keep on praying for you like I do for all these fellas 'round here."

It was like that at the Edge. It was like all life, but free of charge, and everybody was there to share. The young mother returned and fetched both her husband and young son, just in time before the rough crew set in at sundown. Sometimes the language could get deep and dirty.

There were a couple of times in particular when we would be in the shop hours and hours after closing. Snowman, me, and another customer or two, older guys, would share all about our practices, travels to other places, politics, our young people, and music and sports. We'd be there until the early morning hours, howling, fussing, drinking wine, playing dominoes, and scarfing down fresh hot popcorn. On more than several occasions, these guys hipped me to dudes they knew who just skipped out and tuned out, never returned. I thought a lot about that. Maybe I needed to tune out.

This one night, cold as devil's hell, Cool-Nute, Snowman, Big Keith, Nellwood, and I, and three other customers, a few fellas from Jamaica, one a politician of sorts, another a businessman, and a rather quiet Maroon straight from the upper hillsides of the island, dug in really deep. There was of course sports talk, and as always, talk of women, and America's soulmate, racism.

The Jamaican businessman, Roland, I think his name was, started in, his accent heavy. "Now, now, my brothers. Close your eyes with me now, imagine a young professor—his name is Moganstern Hunasti. Yes, I know it's an odd name. His family was strange, too. Imagine yourself being engaged in what he is trying to get you to envision. You all worry too much here in America about the white man." Roland took on playing the role out loud, acting it out. "Racism as an idea gets too much attention, starts to sound like a cliché, and is really not worth all the hype. I call it stupidity. There are really two aspects to racism that ruffle folks, the debilitating bite and sting, hurt, humiliation, and secondly, the insult to your intelligence. Two things will seriously dismantle this: your excellence, and putting yourselves in positions to have access to power by being ready to strike. Power, power!" he said as he raised both his fists in the air. "That's how he teacher us, man." It resonated deeply with us all.

"I was there in the class. I was there, don't you know. He got us with our views on changing directions, ignoring that hate heat. Everything is out here for you, you just have to not get blocked, be a man about it and stay on."

Snowman fell right in on it, "See, yeah, yeah, I told these stiff-tailed St. Paul Negroes that the other day. That's what is meant by power, having the means to execute, to put in place decisions that affect the people. And at the end of the day, nothing will matter if you can't pay your bills, and you ain't getting off your sorry ass. You got to do something, like that dude in here the other day who quit his job, did his own thing. You Island brothers know all about that!"

We all laughed. Snowman continued. "I ain't never known anybody with money that was having severe problems with racism. Getting you to some something down here is the best weapon against stupidity."

Nellwood then shared "You see, with us, in Haiti and other islands, after coming here, having lived through the 60's, 70's, 80's, 90's, and now some years into the 21st century, I can see this in each period. People in most of these communities, through the eras, were concerned and connected to some shared ideas of our common citizenry; people talked about education, housing, political representation, jobs. But today, America is so full of shit stuff. Why? Because the definitions of what's beautiful and Black, virtuous and excellent, prideful and progressive are limited, and even our criteria for what defines who we are is limited. Wasn't like that back then. I feels sorry for these young folk."

Snowman started again. "When you know your history, you excel in excellence, brothers, you know your craft, you are 'bout and 'bout it, like these dumb-bunny hippy- hop kids say nowadays.

Like Malcolm used to say, once you change your thought pattern, you change your attitude. Once you change your attitude, it changes your behavioral patterns, and then you go into some action."

The Jamaican businessman assured everybody there that night he had it all worked out. "Yes, that's how you come to bring something to the table, forget about the past, move ahead. Today, you have to come together on what are the common strategies."

Snowman closed, "That's what I been trying to get you old-ass rust-a-butts around here to see!"

You know, friend, I was in the church, and while I loved the pastor, he never got to the truth quite like these brothers did, really, the deep truth.

The quiet Maroon finally spoke up. What intrigued me about him was his focus on the consciousness, peace of mind, and how to get there. So much of what I was still doing rested upon the doing and not the being. He spoke with such a cool, calmed resonance.

"My brothers, I remember not long ago hearing them on TV, saying "our enemies are innovative and resourceful, and so are we. They never stop thinking about new ways to harm our country and our people and neither do we." This was a President Bush blunder, remember? Then, some militant dudes came back. "No single army in the world will be able to dismantle our resistance." Back and forth with this. I hate listening to the news reports, man! TV is so damn negative. We live in a culture of confrontation and conflict.

"That spirit among us is palpable, like the taste in your mouth after walking through an area with the sickening smell of a dead animal. It's all around us, we drag it with us, carry it everywhere because we stepped in something that stinks. We live under a regime that masks its hegemony and imperialistic arrogance in the name of some kind of a false gift of liberty shared abroad. But the people don't want the gift, man, we would rather return it and have what we had before this sad excuse of a Santa Claus came with this false, idealistic toy." He paused for a moment, and, sensing he had more to say, we waited in silence.

"Studying more closely the life, the spirituality, the commitment, the music, the artistry of Bob Marley once I became a man was very meaningful for me. Of course he is a national hero to us, he was ours. I know the church music man here understands. Music for us is life, encourages meaningful life. In Jamaica, where my people live in the hills, you have to know how that connects so deeply and primarily to the roots, man! We are the work of the African Griots, the healers, the prophet, spiritual advisors, leaders." He began to rise a bit, and it was clearly moving further in the zone of the unfamiliar and uncomfortable for the others, but I was right there with him. The Maroon was talking my talk. He went on. "And notice, in song, it is always the simple poetry that the common community grasps forcibly, the ideas, values. The best examples of this comes from a balance of simple, repetitious, not long, poetry. It's funny, man, you know, how powerful but simple ideas repeated in the depth of style, performance, and sincerity hit and impact. You see this in the grassroots people, roots music like country, Bluegrass folks and dem, blues, spirituals, folk, and gospel, all the time." We didn't need no church this week, the Maroon was on it.

"It's the inner convictions, the voice of the artist, that people inextricably bond with and relate to, the "spiritual consciousness." In the case of John Lennon, Bob Marley, these men were assassination targets, political and social, seen by the people as great leaders. Bob Marley became first a national hero of his people, then an international symbol for what it means to be about peace, peoplehood. John Lennon magnetized a generation with his music and ideas. I often wonder, my curious brothers, what if they knew how to save their embodiment of truth from the spoils of their evil days?" He spoke this directly to me.

Snowman got another cue. "History taught us an ugly lesson, brothers." The popcorn and wine were working the room. "You see that Marley and them, righteous revolutionaries back up there in the days, knew this; that's why they stayed in there, propping up the peoples. Once you paint the people a certain way, as ugly, dumb, or incapable of reason, or having different ideas than yours, having a different approach than yours, it becomes very easy to reduce them to something that deserves less regard. Less consideration, less respect, they become a lesser issue. Yeah, like if y'all read my main man, Ralph Ellison, in his *Invisible Man*—"

Big Keith interrupted, "Yes, Negro, we know who Ralph Ellison is, what's your point?"

Snowman went on, unruffled; he was used to Keith. "That's what I'm trying to tell you, big man with small brain—when you allow somebody to reduce you, they walk right by you, over you, like you're an invisible man. We can't let that happen no more."

Later that evening, I pulled the Maroon off to the side; I felt he understood. I told him, "I get to points where no place, nobody, no God, no man takes me even close to what I seek, or help me get to the truth. They sure ain't here, my brother, they sure ain't here. I fear nothing, and I don't ask nobody for anything anymore. I just want some clarity so I can be at peace, in my mind, deep in my soul."

Marvin, the Maroon, whispered, "Ah, my brother, there are many ways to be sent back from which we all are, and to which you need not look back to, because it calls you forward, if you hear rightly. I know many who have practiced the natural ways to release, and sometimes, understand it or not, deliverance is a better truth."

That day, all the next day, I didn't let go of his methods or his words...deliverance is a better truth, deliverance is a better truth, deliverance is a better truth...

Waiting on Wendy

She sang a colorful alto and had a strong voice. She was considered attractive by these young guys, but she dressed in dark droopy things and kept to herself most of the time.

Like these kids, she wore hooded sweatshirts, so I couldn't really see her face most times. I tried to tell them to dress appropriately, but these days, in these community affairs, church or not, kids never listen. Her clothing allowed her to stay inward despite the outward energy. I could see in her eyes that she searched for something else. She was about nineteen and all over the place with that kind of misdirected self-guided energy common to teenagers. Her name was Wendy Anderson—no relation, different city, different era, but she remained a constant pulse in my consciousness that summoned up Mrs. Anderson.

Wendy was not always paid attention to like all those flirty, flighty sopranos in most choirs. After a few rehearsals, I heard her fingering some sounds at the piano stashed over in the corner, humming to herself and writing down what looked to be a notation, suggesting she was actually writing songs. One day, as I arrived to rehearsal a few minutes early, I noticed she was already there, and she was immersed in reading. I tried not to startle her and began whistling lightly as I approached her. She was reading Ornette Coleman's *Harmolodics*. Of course I took notice.

"Brother Cedrics, I wonder if you can get so free that you escape from your sound. So free you have no place to go." Her intrigue, her honest search pricked at my cold dislike of this generation's musicians. Their songs ring and *cha-ching* about booty and grind, and too much booty and grind ain't much for the mind, and does not get you to the song. The song is what saves. Picasso, though, had said, "In art, there is room for all possibilities," so even among this ragtag motley group of seemingly untalented kids I found a hidden jewel or two. I worked with them with the focus of a fine jeweler, too. Some time after noticing this quiet, hidden talent screaming for discovery, I asked her if she would play a few of her things for me. I don't think she was quite finished with them, but she had some serious potential. I sensed in her not only talent ready to burst, but a real frustration and a struggle to break out from all the stuff that was constricting her. Her family was West Indian, which probably meant parents who pushed her to her limits, albeit with love and zeal. I've known parents like that. That touched me, so I spent more time with her than the others. I knew the worlds she might be trying to balance. What I saw in her was what I missed in myself of late. I had become jaded. I lost my downbeats again and even the church seemed insignificant, a constant daily drain and a drag.

She became trusting of me. She very quietly approached me.

"Brother Cedrics, I want to make something that counts creatively, that counts and connects, that matters. I don't want to wait for these pop people to say what should be listened to. I don't want the fate of my music to be determined by fourteen-year-olds or thugs. I mean, you know, if the fourteen-year-olds and the thugs like it and listen, fine, I'm cool with that. If they don't listen, my music will still sound out in a meaningful way, 'cause I can put it out there myself. I've got a fan base and I tag 'em." She opened her bag further, revealing that she had tapes, sketches, lyrics and whole pile of other stuff, things she'd been working on and wanted to show me. I just jumped in. "What is your passion, Wendy? What is your real deep-down belief about your work?"

"I don't know," she said. "I just want to know I am making *something*. But nobody in my family or friends in my hang really listen to music like I want to. My parents only talk about the payoff, the payoff point. I'm just trying to find my groove, do my thing. Where do

I start?" I didn't know where to begin. She just kept talking, though. "Ornette said he wanted to freely explore the territory that was his musical journey, what he sought."

"Yeah, Wendy, but no matter what, with your creative thing, you have to touch people on your journey as well. The most important ingredient to being successful is how your work connects to people and the world around you. The work of a musician is really tied into and around creative investigation, just like you said with Ornette, and nothing is more important in the life of a musician than this. So ask yourself: what is the potential of your work to touch or move someone else?" I pushed further. "Writing music is really all about a process of organizing your creative impulses, and these ideas are to relate to your experience as a human. This is what music is. Do you have a system for writing down your creative thoughts?"

"Of course, I'm not stupid," she indignantly lashed back.

I didn't think so. She showed me her notations, which were not complete, but showed solid intent. I told her all this all at once—I know I loaded her up, but I had to tell her the music's truth. Usually, all they wanted to know was, "Who made that beat?" to which I responded, "God made the beat. I write the songs," which usually didn't go over too well. Having a young person in front of me who actually wanted to get into music, who seemed to face the same dilemmas I did, I had to give her all the advice I could.

"You know, if you follow your heart and always remember your initial excitement about being a musician, you should never have to worry about music without intuitive inspiration, nor inspiration without a structure and connection, nor structure without cohesion. But before you finish any piece, always, always leave room for the Ghosts."

"The *ghosts*? What does that even mean? I just want to know about me, my thing right now, too much stuff to do out here."

I tried to tell her it wasn't always all about her. "You have to create silence in order to hear what's really inside you. Find someplace quiet where you can withdraw into yourself. That's why you have to leave room for the Ghosts, those things you have taken deep into your soul, the remnants of past inspiration who will instruct you and guide you.

"Being an artist shouldn't be focused on anything else but finding what you are committed to being and expressing in this world. I can't tell you anything more to convince your parents. The things like payoff don't matter; what matters is making a discovery that resonates in the soul and connects to someone else. If the payoff does come, it's only good because it means you've struck a chord, touched others. The true payoff for being creative comes from taking time to explore your inner voice and thought in relation to the world you live in; that's truth."

"Brother Cedrics, I'm too busy making my stuff to get it ready. I don't really know if I have time for all that. I got to get the paper flowing, too."

"Sweetheart, you don't know busy yet, you ain't been down here but 17 minutes. Busy sleeps with me every night under my pillow, whispers in my nightmares to wake up and go." Of course, she shut down after that. My fault.

You know how teenagers build that glacier wall around themselves, hiding from the world? After several months of this push-and-pull game, Wendy's wall began to melt. She became warmer and more receptive to the ideas I was explaining to her. I'm a total sucker for those moments. One day, she pulled down her hood, and I swear an entirely new person was revealed.

"Brother Cedrics, I want to find out who I am, but not just for me." Her eyes, which for the first time I could see were light brown, shimmered, and I could see the thoughts flashing right underneath the surface. She came up really close to me, and whispered, "I need to know now, as a creative person—what am I supposed to live and die for?"

Her question slowed me. This was a question that I could not imagine coming from someone so young. I gave her my best. "That's a good question, my inquisitive friend. What you are willing to live and die for, what you value, that you ask about in your twenties. You have to find that on your own. I can't tell you the answer, but I can tell you what to do with it. You seek it out in your thirties, you believe, live and fight for it in your forties, and beyond that, you better be living in it." Her smile grew as long and wide as the Mississippi. "I got it, Brother Cedrics. I'm on it."

I couldn't help it, but I went on and on. I hadn't had this kind of talk except by myself, with my characters, in years. I'll never know what happened to Wendy Anderson. I think I made one convert, maybe, who knows. Mrs. Anderson always taught us, "Your songs sing when it sounds in someone else's soul." There is an Ysaye Barnwell song that says, "Let my song be a window with an unobstructed view through which you see the spirit in me and I see the spirit in you." I wish I'd written that, but I try and live it. I felt a bit like some old sage, but hey, I had to lay it out for her. The impact I believed I'd had on her made a deep impact on me.

I haven't figured out yet where my journey will take me next, friend. You know me, I'm still traveling.

Ten People

Hope always brews its best soups from the center of chaos.

I saw it coming to a boil. We don't have long with this. While I have a lot of grief for this time I live in, I have more hope to invest in what we could become, and I see it no matter what in the potential of youth. We are restored because of them. All my life, friend, I have worked toward what I believed was holding up the value, the worth of creativity as a renewing of our humanity, and I at every turn saw that creativity being unappreciated, misappropriated, and, in the end, being used to make money or keep people passive, null. Is that what we got these gifts for?

I shared all this with a group at the church after a rehearsal, and, as always, minutes into it, there were fewer young people, leaving just some keen fifty-something-year-olds. Even in the church, the last place I landed, I was finding their interest was in keeping young people occupied and babysat, but not in using their minds to focus on engaging in ideas that change the world they live in.

Today's culture is just short-wired for emotional charges, then they fizzle out. The ten people left standing there seemed pretty enthusiastic, but if I was only there to teach the choir songs, I didn't think I would do that very much longer.

You know, friend, I saw it early on enough to release me. The church wasn't going to get it really, and these kids were not grounded enough in the soils that would allow me to cultivate the good seed of fruiting. I knew I'd have to move along again soon. I had made my decision on my commitments, my last beliefs to be heard. When I thought about the Katrina disaster, I linked that with other inevitable conclusions about the irreversible, chaotic nature of our world. More and more death and war in Afghanistan, Israel, Iraq, Darfur, and even on our streets, in our homes every day. I have had enough of this! This is where the rhetoric of hate has gone in the early decades of the 21st century. "Read my lips" has become "Feel my hate, rage, and watch your own die," a period of war even colder war than we had seen in our lifetimes, certainly since War World II. This is a frightening signal that peace is not at our front doors yet.

Friend, you have sat here with me all night. I thank you for listening.

You know, after you live a few seasons in this thing, you realize everybody has their piece to do, their burdens and their gifts to bear. No apologies necessary, no deals in the end. So you just deal with your pieces on the table and you manage them the best you can. If you can lessen your brother's load, and share a gift or two with your sister, at the end of the day we'll all get there together.

But in this dilemma, what was inescapably human for me was the boundless limits to which life's situations presented themselves. I cannot bear the potential hope of resolving this dilemma, solving that puzzle or that reality on my shoulders alone any longer.

Devonne's Find

Mrs. Anderson continues her tale, addressing the students gathered on her porch.

"After Cedric's last letter came with no return address, I began to worry. He had no parents, no family, no lover that he spoke of. He had told me before that all his life, he had felt like an illegal alien, no matter where he landed. That ghost of his alienation haunted me for months before we found him. Isn't it tragic and interesting how people who are creative walk on a tightrope somewhere between zany, maybe out of their minds, and out of our world, to some necessary deeper consciousness, awareness? I mean, any common person like you and I would be moved off-point dealing with someone like Cedric. Some days, I hear, he was really off-beat. You wonder, is this person kooky, on drugs? Has she or he checked in yet, are they medicated? One like this is a little bit off, well unto themselves and their ideas about the world, and yet a little bit like what each of us wants to become in some way. I think Cedric felt betrayed over and over again because of his undying, yes, naïve faith in the capacity of people, who always let him down.

"I have to save myself from my own depression as I look back on this. Were we to blame? I gave him those initial pushes about his music and what it could mean. We *all* pushed those kids. We never know exactly how our words are taken, how much meaning is attributed to them. For most folks, everything works out alright, settles in, but not for him, it seems. Lord, lord, goodness, goodness, my gracious."

Mrs. Anderson lets her face fall into her hands, overcome by the tears which are now freely flowing. The students watch for a minute as she cries to herself, then wipes her tears away and continues.

"Cedric fell into the cracks of distrust, despair, delusion, and desperately derailed. I remember it well and tragically now, speaking with him a few days after his arrest. All this was normal fare in his mind. But this last time I sensed a simmering loss in his spirit. Of course I couldn't have known he was so badly broken. Who could know, really? Who was there and there to know, to care? After the police released him, he disappeared. I got that letter from him, but then there were months and months where no one heard from him. I just had this emptiness inside, kind of like something had fallen out, one less leaf blowing in the wind. I started a campaign where we sent emails—yes, emails, can you believe this old lady sent emails?—and letters around trying to find out what had happened to Cedric. His cousin, Devonne Divine, was the vanguard, an absolute stanchion. She'd say, "Well, if the sun has to stay up and out, we'll push the clouds back, and squeeze some more light out of that crazy-ass moon till we find him, wherever he's hiding." Oh, here, Devonne printed some emails for y'all to look at."

Mrs. Anderson reaches over to the bag beside her chair and pulls out a few printed sheets of paper.

> *From: Devonne*
> *To: Stephen*
> *Stephen. Glad you received the email. We are trying to find Cedric. Mrs. Anderson and I are worried, haven't heard from the boy in months. Hope these industry thugs haven't done away with him. They're probably trying to stop him for his attacks, writings against the industry through those tracks he sends all around. Have you seen this child, Bonneville? They are all over her! I have to agree with Cedric, crazy as his ass is. It's all turning crap! I sit and watch the music awards shows and I say to myself all the time, "Devonne, they crazy," so you know I*

know what I'm talking about, 'cause I've had this conversation with myself many times, hun. You all have to be kidding me!! They're not listening to me though. Bonneville, they love this child. That girl is screaming, she ain't singing!! It's a mess. Anyway, we will hear a note from Cuz Ced soon I'm sure of it.
Me knows best.
Devonne, and yes, Divine

From: Stephen
To: Devonne

Hi, Devonne.
Girl, you so, is so, has been so, will never be nothing so but crazy.
How you be?
Cedric, yes, my bother must be tripping out there somewhere.
No, I haven't heard anything.
If you do, tell the boy to call us out here or something. He should settle back West. They're crazy out here, just right for him, and it's warm. I can give him some more contacts, if he would just reach out.

Mrs. Anderson resumes her story after letting the kids skim the emails.

"It was through a network of churches that we found out he had been living in St. Paul for months, in one of the communities he had visited over the years. Apparently, he was living in a cheap rented room, showing up at the church, participating in Sunday school, bible study. Funny, Cedric had never really been one for church. What tipped the pastor of that church off was he viewed the denomination " Family find" newsletter. In our description of Cedric, we spoke of his insistence on "music being used to teach the youth." Turns out Cedric had been playing piano and writing songs with the kids and working with the youth minister of this particular church, so this pastor figured it might be our missing Cedric and approached him with the newsletter ad. Cedric knew we were looking for him. For many weeks after that he stayed out of sight. He found out from his landlady, an elderly lady named Mrs. Turner—Sister Paul, they call her—that his cousin Devonne was flying to St. Paul to seek him out. Devonne flew up all the way from California, hoping to catch him at the church during his sessions. These two, Devonne and Mrs. Turner, God be thanked they found each other, since both were critically connected to Cedric. They planned to meet at the Last Stop Ministries church. Now, here's what Devonne told me:

When she arrived at the church, she said, "Hi, Miss Turner, I'm Devonne Divine, so good to meet you in person. How are you? My flight was long, like waiting on Jesus or something. Where is our Cedric? Can I see him?"

Mrs. Turner, an elderly woman was quite warm and anxious to get Devonne to the room that Cedric rented. The two women had decided to meet at the church first, and if Cedric wasn't there for rehearsals, they'd head out to walk to the woman's home a short walk away. Mrs. Turner turned to Devonne and gave her an envelope Cedric had given her. Devonne jammed the note into her purse.

Sister Paul said, "Sometimes, Brother Cedrics—well, I guess that's not his name— Cedric is distant, peaceful, always talking to himself, having conversations. He would say he was just being "creative in his mind." You know, we just love him and think the world of his work with our young people. He spends time with a group of brothers in the church, and they always meet to eat and talk and things. He seems just fine. He gave me that note and said when you got here to be sure to deliver this to you. It seemed odd that he wouldn't want to give it to you himself, but I humor him anyways; we're used to his oddness. He has always been welcome in our home, though. Such a nice young man, real proper and all. He asked me not to worry, but that he needed to be sure you received it, that you would understand. So I took the envelope and he smiled and asked if I'd ever visited his city, that there was a street he lived on called Sturtevant Street. He said he was very fond of his time growing up, and that soon you would be here to visit with him."

Devonne was relieved to know he had been connected with somebody and that he was doing fine, at least up until this point. She wondered why Cedric had chosen this elderly woman to contact her. Why wouldn't he just call?

Devonne spoke. "Well, I thank you for contacting me, let's get to where he is. I tell Cedric all the time to stay connected, I say, "Every minute you think you have you should be thinking of me." Now that I think of it, that line never worked on any of my man friends, so it probably wasn't happenin' for my Cuz either. Me and my Cuz have always been close, so we have been worried of late. There have always been spurts of time where we wouldn't hear from him, but this was the longest. He's always on the move, you know."

As Devonne told her this, they entered the winding stairwell that led to the two boarding rooms of the old woman's home. It was a well-preserved turn-of-the-century Victorian home, with huge pillions on the front steps. Mrs. Turner kept it very nice. The renters entered from the back. In the rear hall entrance, there was a coat rack, a place for shoes, nicely hung, warm, and original oil paintings, and a wooden book case with dozens of classics she offered to her roomers.

"When did you last see him?" Devonne inquired.

"Oh, my lord, it was a few days ago, I reckon. Late one night, he was playing his guitar, sounded like he was writing those songs he worked on, and he poked his head out the door, since he heard me doing my routine sweeping down the back stair wells, they get so dusty, you know. He said, "Hi, Sister Paul, have you heard from my cousin Devonne?" "Yes," I said, "She will be in sometime this week." "Good," he said, "she is the only one I have. She will take good care of me when she arrives." Naturally, I thought he was in need of seeing his family members or something, or maybe there was something he wasn't telling me. None of this is my business, though, I have learned over the years to never get too involved. I tell each of 'em, "Just be respectful, pay your weekly rates, and keep your noise down."" The old lady prattled on. "I have been a member of our church for many years now. My husband and I were born here, in St. Paul, grew up here in this neighborhood. That's why they call me Sister Paul, you know. The church sends me roomers to help keep up my place since my husband passed a few years ago. They have a service that helps people, so they screen the roomers and send them over my way. They have been doing this for decades. It's all by references, and I suppose your cousin knew somebody in the congregation, at least it seems people knew him. Like I said, he seems like such a nice young man, very to himself and into that music of his!"

Devonne responded, "Yes, music has been his world since we were kids. That's all he's ever dreamed about doing. Doing something with people and his music. He's become very obsessed in his adult life. He hasn't been in touch, so you are a blessing for taking care of him and contacting me." While Devonne talked out loud to comfort herself from the frightful suspicions that began to grow in her mind, the note in her purse weighed her down. They approached the top steps and started down a very long hallway. There had been silences before, but this particular one seemed to echo, with a different tone in between the creaks of the wooden steps. As they neared the door, they could hear the Bob Marley songs playing, a good sign that he was perhaps listening, contemplating his next plan, which at times he always shared with Devonne, the only one who would at least listen. Devonne and Mrs. Turner could hear the music, although they didn't hear any stirring, but they caught the scent of the brewed hazelnut coffee which seeped through the hinges and under the door, into the hall, with an irresistible calling.

Mrs. Turner looked at Devonne with a fearful curiosity. After knocking and hearing no answer, Mrs. Turner turned the key and they shuffled through the door. Devonne, seeing her cousin lying motionless, asleep perhaps, and remembering his infectious smile and warm laughter, yearned more than she could understand to hear his thoughts. She shook him.

"Cedric, wake up, Cedric, it's me, Cuz, Devonne Divine!"

But there was no rhythm in his still body. What could have been a very gross and sickening scene was fortunately orchestrated with precise care. Tragic as this was, he, in typical Cedric fashion, was at least kind and poetic enough to himself and all of us to the end. Cedric had bathed, manicured, and perfumed, wrapped himself in his linen robe, put on his slippers, and then sipped the cup of hazelnut coffee he brewed for himself before falling into his last sleep, listening to the music he loved play him into his death. Mrs. Turner, visibly shaken, ran to call for help. Maybe she could have done something earlier, maybe someone could have helped, but it was too late.

Devonne pulled Cedric's note out of her purse, pulling the carefully folded paper out of the envelope.

Dear Devonne.
I know, but you knew too. I am fine. I am happy, at peace, and this was not painful. I just went to sleep. I had been hanging out with some interesting fellows at our local barber shop, and someone hipped me on how to tune out the right way, the final cadence. I have always said it's really about how you find yourself swirling in your storms but then having the freedom to ask and having the sheer delight in getting an answer that comes back to anchor you. There's too much stuff flying around out here! Somebody always throwing stuff at you, all the time. I found my stability now, my calm, the answers came back to me. There are discs of my music, my writings, poems in that bag in the corner. Make sure you give it to people so they will hear. My book never published, Songs For Saving Souls, is for Zach. A brilliant young man, sensitive, with real promise. Please give that to him. He is the future. The discs of songs and tapes of my radio shows go to Wendy, the young lady with talent in the choir.
You should know that this was no casual walk for me. I didn't decide to do this overnight; it's been in the works for a while. Remember Jim Morrison? "Music is your special friend, until the end." I just sat here in these last minutes with my soul comforted by my slowly-brewed coffee. I decided early on I was going set my pace, my tempo in the key I wanted to live in. That's the way I lived my life and it has

been all good for that reason. I've decided my death should be good too. I'm not sad. I have gone away to follow and connect to those sounds I hear beyond us. I think when I get to heaven, the very first thing God should do for me is run and go get my mother. Hey, Devonne, I wrote a poem.

Everybody Gotta Die

*Everybody gotta die.
He, she over there, you, I.
Brother might die.
Friend might die.
Try and understand it?
Why even try?
Love everybody.
Look 'em in the eye.
Hug them.
Say it, "Hey, sis, love you, place no one above you."
In the end what counts and
this we must do, touch, not take
from each other. Touch, give thanks
because in the end. What counts is
what we give lovingly to each other
and this is what matters and what
is truth.
Everybody gotta die.
Live our lives to the end no lie!
Love only tries to keep us on track
on the rail, pushing and pulling through,
giving and making it the best we can do.*

So we keep on hearing, giving, loving each other, yep. She gets on my almost last nerve, hey, but in the end, do it anyway just because, it's " All about Love."

*So brother, I know you hear me, I ain't mad at you.
Dry your tears, don't cry, find your peace now, 'cause everybody gotta die.
Heaven holds those we love.
I love you, Devonne.
Ced*

Devonne dropped the letter, now stained with her tears and imprinted with the crinkles made by her two shaking hands. She began screaming and crying, alone since Mrs. Turner had run to call an ambulance.

This was the day the church would remember as one of their failings, that day Cedric's dissonant torments came to an end—"

Well, that's the way I imagined it might happen in a movie, anyway.

The story Mrs. Anderson *really* told was about how that day, I had breakfast with the pastor, went by the church to water a plant I left there for a parishioner friend who lost his mother. I stroked a few keys on the out-of-tune piano in the cold corner of the fellowship hall where the choir rehearsed. On the street outside the church, I tipped my hat to a few lovely ladies and some homeless men, returned to my room, and closed the door to the world I left waiting to discover. I made my peace with leaving again then left through that door for the last time.

The note was the continuation of my cruel and unforgivable fugue. It just said I had to "go away again." It read, "I am gone." My love for them, though, is as deep as my search. I hadn't died. I just wasn't there, just like before. I was a Ghost for them. They all betrayed me. They didn't care, really. I was simply a story of being away, gone, mad in my own mind and lost in this unforgiving world. I left before they all got there. A foolish waste, perhaps, but I wasn't ready for the act to end just yet. I still have to follow the melody of my soul, regain my mind—my healing is just beginning. I still want clarity.

Mrs. Anderson Closes Shop

The cameras, recorders are still rolling, and they are still wondering about me. The Students are gathered on this last day of filming and being with Mrs. Anderson. This day she seems tired, not much to say. They have been groomed by their professor, enlightened by this woman, connected to a community of personalities who both inspired them and raised more questions among them, and they were truly changed by the encounter with Mr. Cedric. I knew this, I could tell.

I can imagine her every word. I can almost see the sounds coming from her lips as I watch, undetected. She tells them. "You know, life can be like a floating island out there, all by yourself, with no foreseeable connectedness. No lifelines, just out there floating. Yeah, it seems like that, but guess what, it's floating, caught in something that no matter what, sustains that little island. So you got to hold on, hang in, and float through it. You can't push the "run smoothly" button in life. I am finding it's more like a little bit of warm soup, ice cubes down your back, finding a fifty cent piece, then losing your keys. Day by day, prayer by prayer, work to do, live to love, I always say. Life is a precious gift, but you have to unwrap it slowly and not rip it open before you partake in the contents.

"Cedric's been gone away from here for more than 2 years now. We don't know what happened, really, and we have to move on from that. I'm sad about him.

"No matter what you get on the sour side of this life, the fact that you got a life the good Lord gave you should push you to try to fix what you can. Keep working at it, young people, and God will make a way. At least that's what the old folks would say. So, since I am the real old folks now, I can say this with some sense of impunity. In other words, I know I'm right so you just sit there listen. Young people, care for your lives. Treasure who you are and what you got. It's worth all the fight to keep on the track."

Zachekius speaks up, serving the call for his generation yet again.

"Mrs. Anderson, I think we can do that. I know we can even though it might seem that we're not, well, "on beat," as Cedric might say. I mean, I thought he was crazy. Boy was nuts! But I kinda dug what he was getting at with our folks getting to that love piece. I mean, I'm not a musician. I don't rap or nothing, but to live your life to move your people along, hey, you know, that's on point. I'm learning a lot from this book he left me, left us. I'm learning a lot from his ideas."

She stops him. "Do you think he really was committed to those ideas? I always tell young people, don't start a fire then walk away. If you start a fire, turn back around, walk into it, and be committed to blowing it out so that you may salvage something. Cedric starts fires, then leaves without watching them burn. You can't do that. Cedric's beliefs, his passions had been buried deep within. Guess it was simmering and bubbling someplace too deep for us to catch it before it burned him out, ruined him. It's probably the "crazed artist thing." He ain't your map, young people! He was a small bump on your road, which is paved with possibilities. Don't stop believing because Cedric did a dumb thing that night by leaving us all in a lurch, on a search for nothing. What's more important is the ideas he lives for, hoped in. You all live within your ideas and thoughts, but you're committed to living and giving."

The old woman takes a deep breath before continuing.

"I miss him because he was a part of what I hoped the world would be, certainly not how he ended up, a vagabond loose cannon. Cedric's saga has been a betrayal of great promise. We wanted all the kids on Sturtevant Street to succeed, and I have to count our blessings because many of them made it over, turned out pretty normal, doing all right."

She sighs before shaking herself out of it. "Like I said a few days ago when we started this whole thing... how does my hair look, baby? I may still be an old woman, but what I knew then and what I hope for now shouldn't be that far from what you all should be connected to, since, in the scheme of things, I am only you from the past. You need to try harder to hear that sweet reality and see past all the smoke and fire, like I said. That's what I hope y'all will do. Now, Lord, goodness, goodness, I have to get back to my stories."

The Dinner Before, Again

> *When you understand the poignancy, the power of the concept of freedom, it becomes easy to understand the quest for liberation, creativity, spontaneity, spirit, the quest for the expression of truth.*

Then you realize the cost that has been paid for such a state. I don't doubt there are some like you who find this story bizarre. I mean, what sense does it make to never settle, commit and be?

Friend, you know me, right? I had been hanging around that block for weeks and nobody spotted me. That's my story, and that's how I'm giving it to you, just like it was, it is, and it's going to be for now. Truth as a journey couldn't see its end too soon if it were going to be a truth really, right? So I have to find the end, and the search is on.

Love *me*? Puh-lease. They don't love me! They love what they find their comforts to be and I can't be anyone's pillows until I find a place to rest my own head. I'll write them, I'll reach out, and tell them I'm coming home soon, but for now, I'll keep a mailbox where everyone can send me a note. I'm too old now to have a hope in the future, when my eyes are closed. While my eyes are open, I need to get at what I can see and what's in front of me before I trip on it. And if I trip on it, I may stumble into some new thing... I'm still walking.

You getting the check? Thanks, friend. I'll see you around.

Cedric out.

Afterthought

The Negro writer who seeks to function within his race as a purposeful agent has a serious responsibility...called upon to do no less than create values by which his race is to struggle, live and die...create the myths and symbols that inspire a faith in life. It means that in the lives of the negro writers must be found those materials and experiences which will create a meaningful picture of the world today... Surely this is the moment to ask questions, to theorize, to speculate, to wonder out of what materials can a human world be built.

Richard Wright, 1937

    I wanted to write a story from a musician's point of view, of someone growing up immersed in music. It was important to place my main character in a time when culture-shaping events were inextricably bound with the music: the 70's, 80's, 90's. As I began to approach this, rethink, all kinds of images and memories flowered newly in my mind: my dad, mom, uncles, cousins, brothers, and friends; newsreels, TV shows, and past current events, events that were burned into my consciousness as the truth of the world I grew up in, began showing up on the blank pages. That much I could muster up.

    Who are we really unless we get to pursue all we believe possible in life? When I began to think about what this pursuit might be, images flashed immediately in my head. I stepped back into 1967, 1970, 1975, 1980, living on Sturtevant Street. This seems not so distant to me, but as a teacher, I'm aware that most of my students were not born until 2000; they grew up in the context of MTV, cell phones, IPads and iPods, while I, a child in the late sixties, was part of a distant reality TV show called the Civil Rights Era. I call our group, those of us who grew up in the immediate years after the movement, Post-Civil-Rights kids. This sounds like a replacement title for the Baby Boomers, those "old people" who have moved towards retirement towards the last ten years or so. As they are moving, I am, along with my friends, moving to take their places as the middle-aged. I hate the sound of that, but I turned 45 in 2006 when I began to write this novel in earnest. As much as it pains me that I'm creeping nearer to 60, I can't shake away the reality anymore that I am of a different generation than my students.

One of the difficulties we face, which is central to the story, is the negotiation, the navigation of the transfer of values from one generation to the next: 60's to 70's to 80's to 90's to the 21st century, and all the codes, technology, and accoutrements that come with the new generation's world views. All these challenges and confrontations are carried in the music. *The Kids on Sturtevant Street* emerged out of the desire to tell another story through musical narratives, exploring sets of values and stories about a time and people whom I cared about. It's about the dilemma of longing for a past reverence for values that seemed normal, and the longing to be informed by new visions, new outlooks. But then I began to wonder: who really cares about a good-feelings, morals, and values story? Something within the predictable had to turn upside-down so the inner conflict, the real story, could surface. I had to then go and search, invent and compose a more real story that would emerge like a deceptive cadence that resolves in a far-away key. I began to shape my story.

The worlds I love, music, artistry, biography, history, and cultural criticism are all places my imagination and my own narrative roam frequently; they roam those woods of being as a necessity. This novel works out some of that imaginative forest of truth, hope, reveries, and a hope in living life despite the immediate cultural chaos.

CEDRIC'S TRUTH: THE KIDS ON STURTEVANT STREET

Cedric's Truth is a novel, but also a biography, social criticism, a historical polemic, a practical musician's memoir, and a teaching and humanities manifesto. Its form and voice vary to accommodate this fusion of forms and formalities. It's another form entirely. This novel has multiple narrators, including the voices in Cedric's head. The story is told to three listeners: you, the reader, the kids assembled on Mrs. Anderson's porch, and Cedric's friend at the restaurant, who listens to the entirety of the story from the very beginning. As tricky as this format of multi-voice narrative may be, I wanted this book to feel like music; it's a community of speaking voices connecting in harmony.

The looming larger character here is the loosening and loss of Cedric's mind as it unravels, and most of the content of his arguments that fill the page, arguments that drive him into ruin, or perhaps not… *The Kids on Sturtevant Street* is a story about characters who sing in choirs, who harmonize in multiple keys, and who cadence in places unexpected, who compose tunes never heard, and who play in bands everyone wants to groove with, and who occasionally emit a dissonant tone.

Bill Banfield, 2018

About the Author

Bill Banfield, composer, musician author, currently serves as Professor of Africana Studies/ Music and Society, director of the Center for Africana Studies/ Liberal Arts, Berklee College of Music.

He served as a W.E.B. Dubois fellow at Harvard university and was appointed by Toni Morrison to serve as the visiting Atelier Professor, Princeton University. Having served twice as a Pulitzer Prize judge in American music(2010/2016), Banfield is an award winning composer whose symphonies, operas, chamber works have been performed and recorded by major symphonies across the country. Banfield is a national public radio show host, having served as arts and culture correspondent for the Tavis Smiley shows. He has authored 6 books on music, arts and cultural criticism, history and biographies, covering everything from contemporary Black composers, to Ornette Coleman, Nikki Manaj and Kendrick Lamar. In 2010, he was hired by Quincy Jones to write a national music curriculum and book for schools learning about American popular music culture. Dr. Cornel West has called him," one of the last grand Renaissance men in our time..a towering artist, exemplary educator, rigorous scholar, courageous freedom fighter.."